ZHOMBIE
Conspiracy

JEAN FLANIGEN

MARQUETTE BOOKS LLC
5915 S. Regal St., Suite 118B
Spokane, Washington 99223
509-443-7057 (voice) / 509-448-2191 (fax)
books@marquettebooks.com / www.MarquetteBooks.com

In Memory of
Carol Scoggins and Travis Doane

Chapter One

On April 11, 2003 at 1:56 P.M., I was bitten by a black widow spider. That's when I died and I've been dead ever since though you wouldn't guess it by looking at me.

I'm a gardener by trade. Not just any gardener, I use only hand tools. No blowers, no weed eaters, no snarling, shrieking, whiney *noise*. People pay me good money to be quiet here in Carmel-by-the-Sea, California. I also walk. Pretty much everywhere.

If you've never been to Carmel-by-the-Sea, it's little and charming and its streets are insane. Lanes would be the more operative term here. The only thing I'm driving in Carmel-by-the-Sea is a nail. My husband drops me off in the morning and picks me up after my last yard. Sometimes with a lunch date in between.

On April 11, I was edging around a blue aster bed. It was a pretty typical spring day, all cobalt blue, golden and green with mirror bright clouds flashing across the sky. A perfect day to be a gardener; tang of ocean in the air and enough breeze to dry any sweat I might work up.

I was wearing what I call my "uniform" – I'm not being girly here, this matters in the long run – blue denim bib overalls, white shirt, bandanna tied around my neck, boots and a straw hat. Kind of like a scarecrow but my clients like it and we're all part of the tour in Carmel-by-the-Sea. Presentation can make or break you.

I've got my sleeves rolled to just below my elbow, my leather gloves that cinch at the wrist and I'm *on* it. Humming to myself, I'm using edgers to neaten the bottom line when I look down at my right elbow for some reason. There, to my absolute horror, (It still gives me the shudders, even though

I'm dead) etched against the white of my shirt sat a black widow.

Well! Once my heart resumed beating, I jumped up and brushed it as far away from me as I could.

AAH! I didn't see where it *went!* Do you have any idea how many nooks and crannies bib overalls have? (I told you it mattered.) Sorry, I'm glossing over what happened next. It's bad enough the guys working on the house next door got to see it. Suffice it to say that once I determined none of *my* nooks and crannies contained black widow spiders, my shirt and overalls looked like a blue and white puddle at my feet. Luckily, I wear decent underwear when I work! As I was re-attaching the shoulder straps of my overalls, I noticed a tingling in my right arm.

Uh-oh.

I'm alone. The house is empty. My husband isn't due to pick me up for two more hours. Even if I had a cell phone, they don't work here.

Uh-oh.

The tingling is definite and definitely in the crook of my elbow where I could still "see" that dratted spider. Talk about creepy!

I walked, not ran, got my backpack and wrote this note:

1:56 P. M.
Bitten by black
widow spider in
crook of right
elbow.

It was a small notebook.

I set it on top of my pack, all in plain view.

Now here's the crazy part, when things started to get weird. I went back to work! I know, I know, everything says to "immobilize the victim with ice packs on the afflicted area". Then you are supposed to go to the emergency room. No ifs, ands or buts. I went back to work and for the moment, nothing else happened.

See what I mean about weird? *Something* should have happened. Nothing did. No swelling, no shortness of breath, nada.

At least not yet.

* * *

I almost convinced myself that I hadn't been bitten. If it hadn't been for that tingle… I might have. I still feel it, to this day; a burning, aching tingle. As a matter of fact, it's about the only thing I feel any more but I'm getting ahead of myself.

My husband Fleming (his last name) came and picked me up in due course. I told him I was pretty sure I had been bitten by a black widow. His attitude was: you aren't "pretty sure" about things like that. Therefore, I must not have been bitten. Fleming (First name Richard, second name Burton. Which is why he goes by Fleming) is very pragmatic with very little imagination. He couldn't imagine why I hadn't had any symptoms if I had, indeed, been bitten.

For that matter, neither could I.

So, we went on with our lives. We stopped at the grocery store, went home and fed our animals – four cats, two horses – fed ourselves, watched a movie and went to bed.

1:56 A.M. My eyes pop open like some sort of toaster. I notice the time and think, "How dramatic. Exactly twelve hours later. Soap operas have got nothing on me."

I roll over to go back to sleep. Something's wrong, though. I can't put my finger on it; I lie there listening to the night sounds. The clock ticks. (Okay, so I'm old fashioned. I like clocks that tick. Quietly.) A cat snores, Fleming makes no sound. Which is normal, except for every now and again when he lies in a certain position. Then he snores like a freight train and I have to wake him up.

7

A horse snorts outside, a comforting, "I'm safe" sound. Still, something isn't right.

I'm not breathing.

Seriously. Not that I'm holding my breath to listen, I'm not *breathing*. It's now 2:02 A.M. and I don't remember taking a single breath in all those six minutes.

I take a breath, a deep one. I can do it, too, because I'm a singer.

I let it out. Deep, breathe, push out all the old with the diaphragm, then use its natural action to refill the bellows, slow and sure, over and over.

I think, "Okay, I've got it now. Black widow venom is a neurotoxin. The first thing it will do is interfere with breathing. The idea is to stay awake. Make sure I keep breathing."

Did I mention we're both self-employed and don't have medical insurance? We're two of the millions who have "fallen through the cracks" as our politicians so eloquently put it. Did I mention Fleming's a veteran and there are thousands of them in the same boat?

Okay, so we're bitter. I'll just say we're uninsured. I wasn't about to wake Fleming and ask him to take me to the hospital unless it was my last gasp.

Which it wasn't.

I stayed awake the rest of the night. Breathing. I felt like a yoga instructor. In, out, life is our breath, in, out. Basically, I taught myself to breathe by the time the sky began to lighten.

It turned out to be a good thing.

Chapter Two

The rooster that lives behind us has never been able to work out the sunrise shtick. I always say he must have been a lounge act in another life because he never wakes up before nine. He crowed at 9:08 on April 12, 2003. The first day of the dead of my life.

I couldn't believe I had actually nodded off. I was afraid to, so I didn't think I would. Here I was, bright sunny day and still breathing. Inhale, exhale, inhale, exhale.

Fleming was up and out with the horses. The cats put on mealtime shows for them so I had the house to myself. I stretched, reached for my robe and realized I couldn't feel my fingertips. "Okay," I tell myself, "Neurotoxin at work again. I fought it off last night, I'll continue to do so today."

Denial is *so* handy. It kept me going for two weeks. I denied, denied while I traveled to different worlds in what I called dreams. I named it Black Widowland. I never had a bad trip in my life (and the seventies were good to me) until I was bitten by a black widow.

Neurotoxin was my favorite word. Fleming brought me books from the library and I researched the subject dog-eared. I knew so much and so little.

I was devastatingly thirsty, drinking a gallon of water a day without even trying. Food wasn't on the agenda; even my favorite morsels couldn't tempt me. Red wine was. Full, rich red wine. None of that thin, vinegary stuff they sell for $2.99 a bottle. Fruity red wine the color of some fantasy creature's blood.

Out of character! The wine alone should have been setting off alarms in my brain. I'm not an every day drinker. I guess you could say I'm lucky because I have a very definite shut-off point when it comes to alcohol. If I go past it, the results are not pretty. After years of singing in bars, too, a woman's pretty stupid if she doesn't control her drinking. Believe me, I've seen it all. People making fools of themselves in every way possible.

The major tocsin should have been the simple fact of daily consumption. Not normal for me and I'm forty-nine, old enough to know who I am. I hid behind the big D of denial.

Exactly at the end of two weeks, it all stopped. I do mean exactly. 1:56, the works. By this time I was starting to wonder if maybe I'd been kidnapped by aliens. Implanted with some sort of microchip they bought from Bill Gates.

It was all too exact.

I was starting to know it was 1:56 without being anywhere near a clock. The worst of it was, the clock could be wrong… I'd think, "Aha! Off schedule!" … Invariably, my new inner timer was right.

What was I, some sort of Tivo for people from Mars?

Actually, I liked my alien theory. It was warm and fuzzy and I wasn't alone. I had the Martians for company. I was sure they were gathering 'round their sets at home each time 1:56 rolled around to watch "The Lisa Show".

I dilly-dallied, wasting time with that muck in all seriousness while my body slowly died.

The numbness in my fingertips crept up my arms. It took my extremities first and was so insidious I didn't notice the majority of it. I would suddenly realize I couldn't feel something any more.

I have to clarify this "not feeling". Like the tingling, it's not a simple, uncluttered symptom. I don't feel cold, I don't feel pain, I do feel it when Fleming caresses my skin. I also feel my body, its weight and movements. I don't feel heat and worst of all, I don't taste anything.

I say "worst of all" because I used to love food. Not that I was fat; I worked it off. I loved to cook, Julia Child style with real butter, real cream, serving elegant meals to Fleming

10

and I alone. Some of my fondest memories are of meals we shared in our tiny house. We'd toast each other with local wines or water, we didn't care. The food was the showpiece. How we'd savor it, talking over each dish, discussing flavors and techniques. It's so hard to have lost that.

I still eat. I just don't get hungry or taste anything. I could stop eating but I try to maintain a semblance of normalcy.

Because when I finally emerged from denial, I knew I needed to appear normal.

Which I most decidedly was *not*.

* * *

I don't get sick, I don't get tired, I do get bored. I don't need sleep, don't even need to bathe but I do because it soothes me. I made lists, ran tests on myself, wrote stuff everywhere but most of all, I kept it secret.

Fleming, who is a very sound sleeper, didn't wake once during the "night of breathing". He's also not the noticing type and we've been married long enough that we're not aware of each other's every move. Though I missed that crazy-in-love stage, I was grateful now because I was terrified. Fleming did notice the two-week trip to Black Widowland (there wasn't much avoiding that). We had searched with a magnifying glass and eventually found two tiny punctures in the soft skin in the crook of my arm. In Fleming's mind, I had been bitten only deeply enough to inject a small amount of venom. Not enough to kill me, just enough to make me wish it would.

Sounds logical, right? Black widows have weak mandibles and this one had to penetrate my shirt as well as skin.

The big D of denial was still shining brightly for me.

Seeping in slowly, however, was the truth that I was majorly different. I had no theories, no explanations any more. Frozen, afraid to think too much, I went through the motions of my life. I was glad I had taught myself to breathe that first night because I found I didn't need to do that, either.

People *do* notice if you don't breathe for an hour or so. Even if they aren't aware that they notice.

That's how I had to start looking at every single thing my body did or did not do. It might not be a difference people would see but they would *feel* it. That feeling would build over time to a certainty. Certainties lead to Questions and the last thing I wanted was Questions. With the way things were looking from my standpoint, Questions could lead to witch-hunts.

We are only free in this world to be as different as the society in which we live allows.

Get too far outside that and humans are exorcising you or hunting you with flaming sticks. Not that either method works against creatures like me but humans like to feel like they're doing something.

It was all so fantastic; I couldn't deal with it anymore. My mind went on shut down. When I came out of it, I had one thought, crystal clear, left. *I knew about this!* When I was young, in grade school, I had done a report on voodoo.

I was a zhombie.

I simply had to find out who created me and why.

* * *

Being a zhombie was not like what I read all those years ago. "Those books were most assuredly not written by zhombies because they got the simplest of facts wrong," I thought. My skin didn't decay. I'm not a creature of cemeteries or the night. I don't trail grave linens everywhere I go. I lived in my same little house, tended the same yards. I rode my horses in the daylight, sunburned if I stayed out too long and slept soundly each night until 1:56 A.M. My body was exactly the same. Exactly 98.6 degrees, exactly forty heartbeats per minute, exactly the same amount of breaths each minute.

Precisely precise. My skin was soft and flexible where it should be, firm everywhere else. Even my rear end, which had begun to show its age, was now firm, a phenomenon I dubbed the silver lining to the zhombie cloud.

I had no newfound fondness for dead chickens or their blood.

The point is, I am perfectly, exactly, precisely what I should be. I also am not. No amount of exercise accelerates my heart or breathing. I've taught myself to feign breathlessness.

I did develop incredible physical strength.

That part, the books had right. They were full of tales of zhombies ripping through walls or being shot thirty times and stalking off. I could do that.

The first experience I had with my strength was unsettling and almost cost me a livestock gate. We have one gate that has to be lifted as its closed and it's heavy. This gate has always been a struggle for me and broken many a fingernail. On this day in June, I lifted and very nearly tore the gate out of its hinges. Livestock gates are metal and can weigh about eighty pounds. Nothing to Fleming, who was incredibly strong; heavy to me. Unwieldy, too.

I picked up that gate as if it were made of coat hangers. Until I heard the hinges ripping out of the wooden post, I didn't realize I had moved the gate at all. Then I had to run go get tools and repair the hinges. I couldn't let Fleming see it and ask how I had managed to do *that*. Hands shaking, starting at every sound, I quickly reattached the hinges to the post. I was lucky, the damage wasn't too extensive. I had it all repaired by the time Fleming came down the hill for lunch.

Oddly enough, we never had to lift up on that gate again.

However, I had a lot to think about.

The most pressing question was, "Why?" The second was, "Who?" I had no idea who I could have bumped into in my life that first of all, would *want* to do this and second of all, be capable. Who did I know with this kind of power?

Zhombies were made for a reason, too. Usually nefarious. That's not just books and Hollywood. People who work with the white light have no need or desire for zhombies. That's only something the real sick-os do. I honestly didn't think that I knew anyone, ever, *that* messed up...oh.

Maybe I did, after all.

Winston Two-Feathers.

Chapter Three

When I said his name out loud that day in an "Aha!" sort of way, he appeared before me. He scared me so bad, I almost wet my pants. (Yes, I still do that, as long as I eat and drink.) He was so solid and real! None of this holographic vaguely-see-through-him stuff. He was there, standing in my kitchen, odors and all.

I went to SoulJumper (my name for him so I didn't call him to me anymore.) years ago, on a lark. Fleming and I had gone to Omak, Washington to hike in the Pasaytin Wilderness. It's an incredible wilderness, relatively untouched, that stretches across the north central part of Washington, over into Canada. At the time, no motorized vehicles were allowed in the wilderness. We were anticipating a quiet two weeks as far from our everyday world as we could get, mentally and physically.

And get away, we did, for a blissful ten days. We lived with the sun and wind and wild animals. We hiked to spots where a mere whisper sounded like a shout. We drank strong black coffee, sponged off in icy streams and made love under the sky.

When the fire started, we could smell it almost immediately. It was so pristine, any untoward odor stood out. We climbed to the top of the ridge above our camp and spotted the smoke. Not two miles away, as the crow flies and the wind blowing in our direction. Time to hike out.

I guess we were so silly with love, we didn't notice we'd only hiked in six miles before setting up camp. The day we smelled the smoke, we hadn't even left base camp yet. Events were in our favor. Within four hours, we were back in our truck and headed to town. We passed nothing but fire trucks on our way out and we started hearing helicopters and air tankers, so we knew we had made the right decision. We drove to town, congratulating ourselves.

Now I wonder if SoulJumper set that fire just to see what he flushed out of the wilderness.

* * *

We pulled into a motel in Okanogan on Highway 97 next to a casino. Okanogan was a sleepy town attached to the South end of Omak like an afterthought. We could continue our getaway with the added bennie of a little Las Vegas style action. "Little" is the operative word, as the casino wasn't much more than a collection of slots. Not even blackjack but we didn't care. We checked in, unloaded and headed to the coffee shop for a late lunch.

I'm always watching movies and saying, "If they hadn't done that, nothing would have happened and there would be no plot." Finding the pivotal point, as it were.

Walking into that coffee shop in Okanogan, Washington at (you guessed it) 1:56 P.M. was my own personal pivotal point. I know now if I had chosen to gamble instead, the black widow bite would have killed me. I would not be here today.

The question is, would I change it? Give up death-life for death?

I honestly don't know anymore. It's a good thing I didn't have that choice to make.

In we walked. The first person we laid eyes on was SoulJumper. He was kind of hard to miss. The most immediate thing you noticed about him was odor. Not in a bad sense, he smelled like wood smoke and tanned hides.

He tanned deer hide by chewing it, then scrubbing it with urine. He was off the grid; he lived in a tepee on Chopaka, the age-old sacred mountain. The man actually wore hawk feathers in his hair and didn't look idiotic.

With our mind frame, still high in the Pasaytin, he appeared to be the physical manifestation of everything we had just experienced. It seemed *so* karmic.

We sat kitty-corner and across the room but neither of us could tear our eyes from SoulJumper. We wanted so badly to believe. Fleming and I both have been fascinated with Native American ways all our lives. What has evolved is an amalgam of beliefs from a lot of different people. To see the embodiment of our fascination so up close and personal at that specific time was shattering. All our normal walls crumbled. We *so* wanted the vision before us to be an honest-to-goodness Medicine Man.

The waitress gave us a nutshell account of who SoulJumper was and what he could allegedly do for you as she filled our coffee. She was one of his "people". We listened avidly as she plopped containers of fake cream on the table and told us he knew a ceremony to help couples get pregnant.

Ancient, timeless, just like the desire to have a baby. She swore it worked. Wasn't she herself living proof? She showed us snapshots of her two-year-old daughter. Yep, living proof.

Oh, we were hooked, just like the proverbial fish. Ever since high school, when Fleming and I started dating, I'd wanted a little boy with those brown eyes. It was much later, late enough that my biological clock was ringing and we had never succeeded.

We waltzed right up to SoulJumper's table like we didn't have a brain in our heads and made an appointment. Not only did we make an appointment, we agreed to pay him five hundred dollars. In cash. That night. At 1:56 A.M.

* * *

Fleming and I watched TV in our room, got stir crazy, went next door and gambled, anything to pass the time. We thought it odd and symbolic that all night we had such good *luck*. All night we couldn't lose. You can rest assured I don't put any stock in "signs" any more. Luck is luck. You have it when you have it and don't when you don't.

Finally, midnight rolled around and we went to our room to grab jackets and truck keys. We also grabbed a quickie for another kind of luck. Well, maybe not so quick because the digital clock on the nightstand read 12:42 when we closed the door. Warm with love, we didn't notice the cool breeze that had sprung up. Trailing jackets, we chased each other, giggling to the truck.

The logging roads we drove that night were scary enough in the daytime. Slap-happy, we howled with laughter when our heads hit the roof of the truck on a particularly nasty bump. The moon was bright but not so bright as to white out the Aurora Borealis. We talked about being on a ball hurtling through space. Sips of coffee tasted like nectar when we reached an area smooth enough to drink. At last we were there.

Right on time.

The tepee looked like a lantern glowing in the night. I do love tepees – I'm a real sucker for them – and I was drawn to the paintings on the outside. They weren't like anything I'd ever seen. Products of SoulJumper's travels to other worlds, they held no resemblance to anything earthly.

The waitress from the coffee shop, Sharon, crawled out of the tepee and spotted me. "Well, hi! You made it! Have any trouble finding your way? Come on in, tea's made!" She held the tepee flap for me and I happily scrambled in. Tea was, indeed, brewing on a stone close to the fire with the cups nearby. It smelled like Earl Grey, which struck a discordant note.

As Sharon poured tea, I asked where her daughter was.

"Oh, she's in Tonasket, down at the base of the mountain. I don't live up here, I just help out during ceremonies and that." Sharon handed me the steaming mug. "My Grandma, who's eighty-two and still going strong, keeps her for me."

I sipped my tea, savoring the unusual flavor. Nope, not Earl Grey but it did have Bergamot in it. "Sharon, do you blend your own teas?"

That brought a laugh. "No, not me! I buy them from the Co-op in Tonasket." It seemed SoulJumper was the only one who did the primitive life. She herself was thoroughly modern. Computers, microwaves, mortgages, the lot.

Okay, then.

Fleming and SoulJumper crawled in, bringing the fresh night air in a gentle breath. Fleming accepted a cup of tea. SoulJumper chose not to have tea and took a nip from a bottle of whiskey instead.

Wait a minute, wait a minute!

Befuddled as I was, even I knew Medicine Men didn't drink whiskey before a ceremony! I shot a silent message at Fleming with my eyebrows. "Did you pay him?"

"Yes."

Ah. Well, that's what we get for being so honest. Money down the drain, for sure. I took a big slurp of tea and burned the bejeebies out of my mouth. At least that explained the tears. Might as well set my jaw and get through this as best I could. My disappointment was devastating. I glanced at Fleming and could see he felt the same.

What was dorkhead up to over there in the corner? I mean, as close to corners as tepees have. Clutching two turkey feathers, SoulJumper reeled his way back to us.

Why didn't I notice he was so drunk? He had to have been drunk when we arrived, to be so far gone now. How could I, someone who had sung in bars for years, not have identified the situation? I had serious doubts about my drunk-o-meter, usually so accurate. My mental needles should have been off the scale! I blamed myself for being dreamy with an over-active imagination.

Sharon was pulling a drum out of a stack of hides. At least it looked like a native drum. It was a bit incongruous, seeing this bleached blonde smacking gum, extra-long cigarette in one hand, beating the drum with the other. Her shirt said, "See Rock City" and I wondered idly how in the world she had gotten hold of it. She didn't seem that well traveled and I doubted if she'd been beyond the county line, much less to Tennessee.

SoulJumper began to chant in time with the drum. At least he had that part together! As Fleming and I sat on cheap metal folding chairs (probably stolen from a local church) and watched in dismay, SoulJumper and Sharon made a mockery of our dreams. We should have known better but we didn't. It was so awful.

SoulJumper staggered between us and the tepee fire, using the turkey feathers to waft puffs of smoke at us.

Sharon chewed and smoked and beat the drum boomboomboom as our hearts shriveled. SoulJumper chanted, the ooga-ooga-unga you heard in old Westerns when they always used the whitest people to play the natives. He smeared ashes from the edge of the fire on his cheeks, then Fleming's, then mine. A few more staggers and reels, a couple more puffs of smoke and he was done.

Done is right! How bogus could you get? If there were a Better Business Bureau for Medicine Men, this guy would be *reported*. Eight o'clock in the morning, sharp!

Sharon set the drum aside, took a deep drag from her cigarette and sneered at me through the smoke. SoulJumper staggered to another pile of hides, fell down and to all appearances, passed out.

By this time, my anguish had turned to fury. I got up, stalked over to Sharon and slapped her, hard as I could in the face. Without a hitch, she took another drag. As the smoke curled around her head, she slitted her eyes at me. Her lips didn't appear to move as she said calmly, "You'll be sorry you did that. Now get out."

No problem.

Chapter Four

It was a quiet drive to Okanogan. Whenever the road allowed, we clutched each other's hands like little kids. As we pulled into our parking slot in front of our room, I started to apologize. And cry. I hate it when that happens, I want so much to act logical but I never can. Fleming is such a dear when I do really lose it. He wipes my eyes, my nose and doesn't mind me crying all over any shirt he owns. He pats me and comforts me, even if I was wrong and don't deserve it.

Which is what he did.

When I had stopped slobbering and jabbering, he came around and opened my door. "Come on, sweetie, let's go get some sleep. Then we'll decide what to do."

That was right. We still had three days of vacay. Not that we felt like it but it was still there.

The next morning was cloudy, like us. We braved the coffee shop even though we both quailed at the thought of bumping into Sharon and SoulJumper. We still had a little luck left over because Sharon was on the afternoon shift. SoulJumper was probably lying in his tepee nursing a hangover with a little hair of the dog.

As we stood at the cash register paying our bill, we noticed a promotional flyer for Leavenworth, Washington, a Bavarian style town in the Cascades. It was out of there and we could still hike if we chose. The place even had a train we could take through the most rugged parts of the Cascades to Seattle.

We left Okanogan without a spared tear or backward glance.

* * *

We never did have that little boy, so we have horses and cats instead. As a matter of fact, we came home from that trip and found our two horses almost immediately. Exquisite Arabians, gelding and mare, with the same sire. The cats came to us willy-nilly and stayed. Cats can sense cat people from miles away and are not fool enough to leave a sweet deal.

We built our "family" and our businesses; Lisa the gardener and Fleming the mechanic. I sang whenever a gig came my way. Tending our garden eased the pain and left us tired at night so we could sleep. I guess we grew apart in this time. We both had our thoughts. I took many an early morning ride, moving through the swirling mist. It was such an obvious metaphor for how we felt, we embraced it, Fleming and I. But we embraced it separately.

We had lost the de-coder to our communication.

We still had our love and shared life. It was just more like good friends. We shoveled manure together, cooked together, even made love but we no longer laughed together. That silly, fluffy, we're-so-happy-together laughter was gone and it seemed like it wasn't coming back. The childhood of our marriage was over.

Of course, we had Responsibilities. That's what we told ourselves if we gave it any thought at all. We bought our two acres and tiny house in Carmel Valley instead of renting as before. Our landlord offered and we discussed it, agreeing easily it was the Right Thing To Do. We had horses to think about. Horses are quite the Responsibility. I'm surprised we didn't buy a minivan! Luckily, we had no use for one; I was spared that particular societal cloning.

We did buy an older four-wheel drive truck to pull the horse trailer we bought because we bought the horses…

You get the idea. One purchase begets another. It's called nesting. We drifted along. Until April 11, 2003 at 1:56 P.M.

* * *

Now that I was aware of who had made me a zhombie, I wanted to know how. I racked my brain, going over that scant two hours in a tepee on Chopaka. I could not figure out how SoulJumper had managed to make me zhombie. I was still thinking inside the box. Theses are, indeed, modern times. Even for those of us who choose to live off the grid.

It's called DNA.

Saliva, on the rim of my teacup.

Yeah.

SoulJumper had a friend with a lab. His friend isolated the DNA for him and right there, in the lab, he made me. The tricky part is knowing how to walk in several worlds at once. It's called the theory of parallel time. Everything's all happening at once. It *is* all happening at once. Very confusing until you get the hang of it.

Put very simply, SoulJumper went into parallel times and worlds and used my DNA to bring me back and make me immortal when I died from the black widow bite. Because I *did* die. Within thirty minutes of that bite, I was deader than a doornail. SoulJumper brought me back.

Now I was irate.

Actually, it felt kind of good to feel *some* emotion after all the years of floating. Zhombies do feel emotion just not quite the way humans do. It's more distant; less overwhelming but there, nonetheless.

SoulJumper had an angry zhombie on his hands.

Trouble was, he controlled me. Remember I said I slept every night until 1:56 A.M.? That's when SoulJumper took over. At first, he merely showed me my new world. Come to find out Sharon was a zhombie. She laughed and laughed when I showed up with SoulJumper.

Mainly we traveled through time at first, then expanded to galaxies. If someone human could harness this mode of travel, airlines and car manufacturers would soon be out of business. You just think yourself there. You picture where you want to go and you're there. Really there, all three dimensions of you.

The first couple of times I tried it, I squinted and pursed my lips and practically laid an egg. Naturally, it didn't work. It's actually very effortless.

I had a real love/hate relationship with SoulJumper at this time. I hated him for making me a zhombie but on the other hand, he was the only one who could show me how to live as a zhombie.

I had to tell Fleming.

Oh boy. Mr. No-imagination, imagine *this*. You have a zhombie for a wife! Sure. I tried to cook him his favorite dinner. The old way-to-a-man's-heart theory. Trouble was, now I couldn't taste anything, I couldn't cook, either! Sorry state of affairs but there it was. Even a roasted chicken with herbs from our garden – one of my standbys – came out tasting too herby. We ordered pizza from a place at mid-valley and sat in front of the fire to eat.

Great. Now what?

Just how do you say, "Honey, I'm a zhombie," without sounding like a bad horror flick? No matter how you word it, it sounds melodramatic. At length, I started with April 11. I asked Fleming if he had noticed any change in me.

That's when the poor fellow started to cry!

Surprised the daylights out of me! I mean, not that he never cries but his timing seemed a bit odd. He was crying hard, too, hiccing when he breathed in and trying to catch the tears with his fingers.

I went over and put my arms around him the way he's done for me so many times. I had on my best silk blouse but there are things more important in life than even the most flattering blouse. I brushed Fleming's hair out of his eyes and he looked at me like a soulful deer. I kissed the tip of my finger and put the kiss on his lips – a little something we used to do when love was young. "What is it, honey?"

Fleming looked away, tears still leaking from the corner of his eye, drop, drop. "Where do you go every morning?"

I was nonplussed. This, I had not expected. I tried a diversion. "You mean my rides?"

Fleming gave me his why-do-you-try-to-hide-anything-when-I-know-you-so-well look and said wearily, "No."

Ah.

Fleming straightened in his chair and looking at the fire, he said mechanically, "Every morning at 2 A.M. you leave. You don't come back until 6. Where do you go?"

"1:56 A.M., actually." I said it stupidly, without even thinking.

Fleming turned his head to me. His eyes flashed in anger. "And what is it with you and 156 these days? Do you know how many times I've heard you say those three numbers, in that order lately? Is that your new boyfriend's apartment number or something?"

I almost laughed. Thank goodness, I had more self control this time and managed not to. "Sweetie, I am not having an affair." Understatement of the year!

Fleming just looked at me. And waited.

So I blurted it out. Not in any semblance of order at first but finally I was coherent enough to make Fleming understand. The trouble was, he believed me. I think all this time, I was waiting to tell Fleming and have him say roundly, "Nonsense!" I must have still had a place in my heart that thought Fleming could fix this, make it all go away. It hit me at that moment, when I saw comprehension, believing in my love's eyes that no one could fix me, ever again.

I was a zhombie and always would be.

Chapter Five

Fleming wanted to go after SoulJumper. We both used that name for him after I explained to Fleming that we called him to us every time we said his name. Fleming wanted his *hide*. He also realized it was not something that could be done in this world. You can't exactly walk into a police station and say, "I want you to arrest this guy because he turned me into a zhombie." I wasn't powerful enough yet to fight SoulJumper on his own turf. We decided to bide our time. I needed to learn more about the ins and outs of zhombie-dom. I'd let SoulJumper teach me and we could use that knowledge against him down the line. Fleming would cover for me in the human world whenever necessary and take notes.

I began to "download" everything I learned with SoulJumper to Fleming on my return. We figured very little was known about zhombies, so a little documentation couldn't hurt. Might even help us figure a few things out.

Then I started to disappear at 1:56 *P.M.*

It was a good thing I had filled Fleming in because the daytime disappearances required a plan. I disappeared at 1:56 P.M. and came back at 5:56 P.M. Now we had to make sure I wasn't doing anything important when it happened. Once, I was at the grocery store, next in the checkout line with a full basket. I walked out, left my purse and everything. I could hear the checker calling me but I had no power to stop or turn around. Fortunately, the checker knew us and returned my purse. We told her I had a stomach virus and was getting ready to hurl so I had to get out of there.

I'm glad no one saw me dematerialize. That would have been a little harder to explain.

My lessons with SoulJumper had changed, too. Now I was learning to rearrange reality. What humans know as reality is an illusion. Reality, as we here on Earth perceive it is a collective illusion, kind of like group hypnosis. Time is light and can be bent and formed. I was learning how to alter the human world from behind the scenes. I was also learning to walk in more than one world at a time. You kind of flatten your essence into a couple of time lines and be in both at once. In a way, it's sort of like being a kid and learning not to tell lies because it's too hard to keep up with what you've told people. Only, in this instance, you have to keep up with all of it. Sort of happens outside consciousness but inside it as well.

I still hadn't figured out why SoulJumper had made me in the first place. Fleming and I had countless discussions about why I was chosen, not he. I said it was because SoulJumper wanted a zhombie harem. Fleming said it was because women have more psychic power. Neither one of us was correct.

SoulJumper needed a succubus.

* * *

I never was the most sexually extroverted person in the world. I fell in love with Fleming at a young age, giving heart and virginity pretty much at the same time. He was my one and only and always will be. We had a wonderful time, exploring our sexuality together. I never so much as glanced at another man – didn't even ogle movie stars – I never needed to. My sweet Fleming and I made magic together, even in the frozen years. You might say I was naïve. I had never once known sex without love.

Enter SoulJumper. Talk about a nefarious plan, the guy was a pimp!

Uh-huh.

It's just that his clients didn't know the prostitutes they paid dearly for were dead. Imagine – hookers who can travel anywhere, at any time in history or the future, under complete control of the pimp. And not costing him a dime.

Sweet. For the pimp, anyway. I was the last zhombie SoulJumper made, the last one he needed. I completed his plan.

* * *

When a zhombie is made the crucial time – the time of control – is always the time the zhombie maker first laid eyes on the victim. Therefore, 1:56 for me. A.M. or P.M. it doesn't matter. Initially, the control lasts four hours. SoulJumper owned eight hours out of twenty-four of each zhombie he created. Starting to see a pattern?

SoulJumper operated an international, intra-world, inter-time prostitution ring everywhere at once. It gets tricky but he was very accomplished – the drunken stunt in the tepee was a ruse so we would underestimate him – and could walk in eight worlds at once. And achieve three-dimensional solidarity in all of them.

I was up to two. Has a ripple effect, doesn't it? There were eight of us. One for each world SoulJumper walked. Where ever he walked. His primary target in this world was Asia. Each of us had a special "appeal". One zhombie SoulJumper created was only eight years old. I'd have murdered him when I found out about her if I could've figured out how.

I was the motherly type. I think it made it easier for me because that's all a lot of my johns wanted – mothering. A few wanted to be diapered and bottle-fed. The worst were the guys (or women) who had issues about Mom. They could be brutal. When you don't feel pain or bleed, a little more money makes it all right, doesn't it? SoulJumper didn't even need to worry when a john beat us up. He collected more and went on his merry way.

Being under a zhombie maker's control is a lot like being hypnotized. Your body does things while a part of your mind

28

looks on and says, "I shouldn't be allowing this." The whole time I was storing memories. They seemed distant, as if I were watching someone else but they were there. I had quite the catalogue of horrors when it dawned on me SoulJumper had no master. How did he manage that?

It was time to find out.

Chapter Six

Poor Fleming. When I think about what he must have gone through in this time … I was still downloading to Fleming on each return. He knew about it all. I tried to spare him the worst of the details but for some reason the man suddenly developed an imagination. If I didn't tell him what happened, he dreamed up a lot worse. I think he was happier than me when I came back and said, "I think there may be a way to destroy SoulJumper."

I had just had one doozy of a night. One of my tricks was in ancient Japan, some minor ruler. This one must have had a real gem of a mother and in that day they didn't hold women in the highest regard. He began with pinching, which escalated to hitting. When he punched me in the face and nothing happened, he began to scream.

A part of me is watching the scene, comprehending. The rest of me is unable to leave until the control time is up or SoulJumper releases me. The guy is going ballistic. I don't speak that much Japanese; only the few words necessary in my "trade" but any fool could see he was screaming for servants. I could hear doors sliding open and the pattering of running feet when SoulJumper finally showed his useless face.

He took me to the tepee on Chopaka. I looked around, my lip curling in disgust. "Charming." No response. SoulJumper began to build a fire. He couldn't have cared less how I felt. I stared fixedly at him. "There's no telling what those people would have done to try to kill me."

SoulJumper smiled a tight-lipped smile and said, singsong, "Well, it just wouldn't have worked, would it?" His voice normal again, he went on, "Besides, you gave them material for their legends."

I sat down on one of those bedraggled folding chairs and snarled, "A hooker to the Prince, who, by the way, has serious Mama issues (Princie, that is) and this hooker doesn't bruise or bleed. Or lose teeth when you punch them out. That's the stuff of legends, all right."

SoulJumper snorted. "You always did have a way of putting things, Lisa."

I still had an hour, Earth time, before my control time was up. I wondered what SoulJumper had up his sleeve for me now. Probably something icky. I sat there, trying my best to be part of the furniture, pondering control times. Out of the blue, I asked SoulJumper when his control times were. I mean, the way he explained it to me originally, zhombie-dom is a real pyramid scheme. Every zhombie has a master because someone had to make them.

"I don't got no steenking control times."

Beg your pardon?

"Whaddoyamean no control times? I thought every zhombie had control times."

"That's what you get for thinking when you're not used to it."

I waited. If SoulJumper has a fatal flaw, it's his need to flap his jaws about how smart he is. The fire popped. Outside in the chicken coop a chicken began to squawk, laying an egg. A jet flew over.

"I'm not a zhombie."

I *knew* I'd get him!

* * *

The next second, I was home in bed with Fleming. It was inconvenient but I knew I'd get more out of SoulJumper. Was he immortal? Exactly what kind of power did he have? I'd always assumed he was a zhombie.

Fleming rolled over, yawning. "Okay, sweets?"

"There may be a way to destroy SoulJumper."

31

Fleming raised up on one elbow. "Really?"

I smiled. "Really" was one of our love code words. He would say, "I love you" and I'd say, "Really?" Then I'd say, "I love you" and he'd say, "*Really.*" Silly things married people do but we treasure them.

"Yes, my darling, really. He's not a zhombie."

Fleming's eyes flew open at that. "Is he immortal?"

"Great minds think alike, hon. My question exactly."

We sat there, side by side, thinking. Fleming was the first to speak. "How did you find this out?"

"Why don't we go into the kitchen and I'll tell you while I make coffee."

As coffee perked, Fleming and I leaned on the sink and munched day-old doughnuts while I filled him in. Fleming loved stale doughnuts and they could have been a week old for all I could tell. I was only eating because it was a shared moment with my husband.

"This is vital knowledge he shouldn't have given me," I said somewhat indistinctly, spewing puffs of powdered sugar as I spoke. "He sent me home early as soon as he told me. I still had another forty-five minutes of control time. He freaked out because he shot off his mouth and shipped me right out. We're on to something, Fleming."

Fleming chewed and watched the sky turn from inky blue to indigo outside the window above the sink. "Coffee done?"

I poured coffee without speaking. Fleming needed time to think. When he had worked it all out, he would tell me what was up. I handed him his mug and he said, "Let's go build a fire."

Whoa. This was deep. Not only did he need more time to think but we did our best thinking in front of that fire. Some of our best loving, too! We settled into our armchairs and watched flame crackle through kindling. I had a wild thought. "I wonder if those people would have tried to burn me?" Thank goodness I didn't blurt it out! If I could have cried, I would have broken down, then and there. That's when it hit me for the first time, full in the face, what I was.

I was a monster.

The Prince and his menservants couldn't have even injured me, granted. But I was a monster. Rouse the townsfolk, call a priest. I looked down the long, lonely hallway of immortality and wanted nothing more at that moment than to be able to die.

Lifetimes of freakdom.

I was going to *kill* SoulJumper!

* * *

Fleming was still lost in thought and didn't notice my mental disarray. Zhombies don't send out "vibes" and we had lost our nonverbal communication. Maybe not lost, precisely, because we had learned a new form. Like blind people develop better hearing, we had found a way to compensate. I was glad he hadn't noticed me bottoming out, though. I still hadn't downloaded to him and he appeared to have forgotten about it. I knew he'd remember eventually but let him go on in blissful ignorance as long as possible. I looked at all Fleming's new gray hair glinting in the firelight. He had aged. I wished there were a way I could snatch time back for him. I knew how to do so much with time now. Why couldn't I save my love?

I *really* needed to get off this train of thought! Boy, was I moody today. I wondered if there was such a thing as a menopausal zhombie.

Fleming stirred and cleared his throat. I smiled at him, mentally buttoning down the hatches. Don't let any awfulness leak out.

"Do you think Sharon or any of the others would be any help?"

I blinked at my brilliant husband. I had never questioned how the other "girls" felt. Especially Anna, the eight year old.

33

I only knew about two of SoulJumper's other zhombies, Sharon and Anna. The other five were still a mystery.

Oh, this had possibilities!

Chapter Seven

Zhombies can be very useful for people with evil intentions. There is an entire world that exists in the shadows of the one most humans experience. This is where nightmares are created and insanity is bred. SoulJumper's use of zhombies for prostitutes was foul enough but there were worse. A lot worse. Zhombies make ideal assassins. Totally unidentifiable, nothing gives them away. Simply travel through time, take care of business and off again. Zhombies also make effective house haunters, stepping in and out of worlds to create paranormal phenomena. Fragile minds have been sent tumbling and kingdoms seized because of zhombies' abilities in the space/time continuum.

There's nothing supernatural about what zhombies do – except immortality, of course – we simply know how to work with energy. Not only in our universe but every one we enter. Have you ever heard of the perfect alibi? Of course you have. A murder is committed. A suspect is spotted at the scene but the same suspect is across town having dinner with friends at the time of the murder. Simple enough, if you're a zhombie, by walking in two time lines, minutes apart, at the same time.

The person sitting next to you on the bus could be one of us. No pallor or fangs or blood thirst to hide. We don't have to avoid the sun or worry about subnormal body temperature or garlic. We fit right in.

Naturally, it's not that easy to make a zhombie. Nowadays it takes an immense amount of money and a full laboratory with some ancient knowledge thrown in. Like a box of laundry soap, we are new and improved. Even those of us living in the supernatural world keep up with the times. I discovered those old books were more accurate than I thought. Zhombies did look like decaying cadavers until the advent of cloning. Using DNA made it possible to make us appear human. With practice, a zhombie can live centuries without discovery.

How in the world did SoulJumper get involved? He had a shrewd wit but I didn't think he was capable of extensive scientific deduction. He had his fingers in economic pies all over the world but that didn't take brilliance, only smart accounting and an almost feral ability to sniff out an idea that was a winner. The gold coins and antique treasures his "girls" earned from every period of history kept him in high cotton. SoulJumper had even taken advantage of a couple of inventions from the future; patenting them days before they were invented.

He couldn't give a hoot about changing history or the future. He went by the theory that no one would ever know it was supposed to be different. I have to admit, once you start traveling through times and worlds and you discover alternate realities – time lines that kept going after human reality changed course – it is harder to be concerned about altering the course of history. There are a myriad of alternate realities for every second that we live. Sort of like mirrors that show several angles of an image at once. It's easy to think history shouldn't be changed when unaware of all the versions of history that exist echoing through time, every bit as valid as the version we are in at that moment.

That still didn't excuse SoulJumper messing up people's lives the way he did.

To tell the truth, I felt no sympathy for the johns. Anyone who thought of sex as a commodity had to take whatever came with that, in my mind.

Especially sex with eight-year-old girls.

It was time to find a way to talk to Anna.

* * *

Zhombies may not have full human emotion but if in life you basically knew right from wrong and had certain morals, you stayed that way. We also have excellent memories. I knew what it felt like to come back to my life twice a day – all healthy and normal and full of love – with the memories. Dark, ugly, sick memories. Growing fungus in my mind. I wondered how Anna felt about hers.

Fleming had me thinking furiously. I didn't know if Sharon would be with us. She was the closest of all to SoulJumper and seemed to like him well enough. As much as she liked anyone. Her persona was the seasoned prostitute with the soft heart. She knew every sexual game and toy in the book and people that liked hookers got her. She knew how to make them shiver in their shoes and had a regular stable of admirers of her technique. I felt I needed Sharon to get to Anna, though.

Who was Sharon before being made a zhombie? Would she help me destroy SoulJumper? I didn't think I'd be able to fool Sharon into thinking I had an innocent reason to talk to Anna. We had nothing in common on the surface, Anna and I. Anna was an eight-year-old black girl from Detroit and I was a forty-nine year old white woman from the cushy Monterey Peninsula. The only unifying factor was SoulJumper. Sharon would guess. She knew how much I hated him. I wondered if Sharon still worked at the coffee shop in Okanogan.

I glanced over at Fleming waiting patiently, staring at the fire and said, "We'll have to start with Sharon and it will have to be in this world."

Fleming murmured, "You need to find out when her control times are. It would be easier if they were close to yours."

I took a swallow of coffee. Bleh. Worse than usual. Must be cold. I set it on the hearth to warm. "Now I'm thinking of it, our control times might even overlap. I'm always seeing her in other worlds."

"How long has she been a zhombie?"

"You know, Fleming, I have no idea. I never thought about that."

Fleming leaned forward to flick a spark back where it belonged. "It might make a difference. Kind of a seniority, if you will. She might know about powers you haven't been introduced to yet."

I sighed. "The issue is, how does she feel about being a zhombie prostitute? How does she feel about SoulJumper? I can't imagine anyone being content, being controlled by him."

"Do you have any idea what her last name could be?" Fleming set his coffee next to mine. If I was a halfway decent wife, I'd get him a fresh cup. I settled deeper in my chair. Even zhombies can be childish. Besides, I didn't want to interrupt the train of thought by leaving the room.

Fleming got up and fetched the coffee pot from the kitchen. He poured fresh coffee into both our cups and left the pot on the hearth so we wouldn't have to get up again. Now I did feel like a rat! "Need another doughnut, sweetie?"

Fleming shook his head. "So? Do you know Sharon's last name?" He smiled gently, knowing everything that had crossed my mind.

I smiled back sheepishly. "No. Never have heard it."

"I wonder if she still works in the coffee shop."

It was no surprise to me that I was still so crazy about Fleming. Not only were we on the same page, he was coming with me. "I don't know. She told me she lived in Tonasket, though. It's tiny. It can't be that hard to find her."

"We'll need to change the oil in the truck."

Chapter Eight

It took us two days to get ourselves together for the trip. Then two days to drive to Tonasket. We stopped at a convenience store on the main drag that had a few motel rooms stashed behind it. Fleming went in to ask about rooms while I held onto the truck and stretched out the road kinks.

Fleming returned too quickly. "No rooms, honey. We can drive back to Okanogan or the lady inside has a cabin on her property we can rent for the night. It's just south of here, right off 97."

"Imagine that."

Fleming grinned. "Quite the coincidence."

"How much?"

"Pretty fair, actually. $50.00 a night."

I leveled an eye at Fleming. "Does this cabin have indoor plumbing?"

We laughed out loud at that. It didn't matter to me anymore but I used to be very picky. If I was prepared for dry camping, fine. If I was packed for a motel room, I wanted indoor plumbing. "Actually, no. Does it matter?"

We both sobered. So many reminders, every day, that we were no longer the same. I shook my head with a sad smile. "No, sweetie, it doesn't."

Fleming grabbed my head and ran his knuckles over it. Scobbing your knob, he called it. "Come on, then!" Swinging our hands between us the way we did when we walked the halls of high school, we entered the convenience store.

A lady with unusually red hair took our money (cash) and wrote us a receipt on a napkin. She handed us a key on a frayed piece of green yarn as she gave us directions. It didn't sound too awfully hard, which was a blessing since we were already losing daylight.

Thirty minutes later, we turned off the truck in front of a tiny board and batten cabin. It looked as if a good wind would carry it off but it had charm. You couldn't even see any other house lights from it. When it came to privacy, you couldn't beat it. Best of all, it had a huge old Ponderosa pine standing guard over it, red bark glowing in the last day's light. Laden with overnight cases and grocery bags, we stumbled across the uneven ground.

The front door was low – Fleming would have to remember that or he'd be cracking his head – and stooping and bumping luggage we practically fell inside. It *was* cute. The inside was solid wood. Tongue and groove paneling, open rafters, rough wood floor. One large room contained a double bed, a dinette set with two chairs, a wardrobe, a couch and a wood stove. The bedspread and matching curtains were brick red with brown bears pacing across the bottom. The dinette set was tacky but hey, I could live with it. Maybe we'd stay here longer than one night.

That is, if we didn't find Sharon right away.

* * *

We munched on junk food from the convenience store. The temperature was dropping but we were toasty. Even had a window open for fresh air. Fleming had discovered a stone fire pit in back and we built a fire there, too. When Fleming was full, we wandered outside with the chairs from the dinette set.

We watched the stars, our breath making clouds as we talked softly.

Our marriage was different now. We no longer made love – understandably, Fleming had issues about that. Our friendship had deepened. Something this horrible could make or break us. It made a new us. I often wondered about

Fleming's future, though. How would we be able to weather his aging while I stayed eternally the same? And what about when he died? What then?

SoulJumper taught me as a non-dead, I had no access to the dead. We were like proverbial ships passing in the night out there in the universe. I was no more than a whisper – a fleeting impression – to the legitimately deceased. How would I deal with Fleming leaving and never, ever being able to follow?

I definitely needed to find out if there was a way to un-zhombie somebody. I just didn't know who to ask. Zhombie knowledge is all, without exception, passed down verbally. Anything written is subject to discovery. If a zhombie's maker chooses not to share information, nine times out of ten, the zhombie exists in ignorance. Naturally, SoulJumper had no interest in sharing with me how to free myself.

Fleming yawned and got up, stepping into the sagebrush to relieve himself. Men are definitely plumbed for the outdoors. They've got it all over women in that department. I always kidded Fleming he was like a dog, marking his turf. I'd tell him, "Be sure and get all the perimeters, honey."

All of a sudden, I heard Fleming yell, *"Lisa!"* He came tearing out of the sagebrush, looked right through me and ran past, into the darkness beyond the cabin.

That was the last time I saw my sweet husband's face in this world.

* * *

I ran after Fleming calling, calling but he never heard. Where were my stupid powers now? Sometimes zhombies are only too human.

I couldn't catch him, couldn't stop him. The moonlight was bright so I was surprised when he disappeared. I almost went off behind him. I caught a juniper branch just in time and felt by body sail out over open space.

41

There was a cliff, straight down, a thousand feet or more. No indication from our side, a gentle slope up and – you're airborne. My love never had a chance.

I named that cliff Lifetaker.

Chapter Nine

The next morning on a clear sunlit day, sparkling with life, I watched the paramedics take my love away. A gray bundle now, strapped to a gurney. My being crumbled as they rolled the gurney in the ambulance and closed the doors.

So final.

The Sheriff standing next to me cleared his throat. A nice man, not very well versed in grief. Lucky guy.

"Your husband went out into the sagebrush and never came back, is that right, Ma'am?"

"Yes," I parroted for the fourth time. It didn't matter, he could ask me the same thing a thousand times to check my story. I had no feeling left. I nodded. "Yes. I called. When he didn't answer, I grabbed a flashlight and went to look. I don't know why he got so far from the cabin, unless he got lost."

The Sheriff tried not to show on his face what he thought of stupid city slickers who went out at night in unfamiliar territory without a light. "You found him at the bottom of the cliff?" Skeptically.

"Not until sunrise. I spotted his shirt." Red, against the gray of the rocks. A special, expensive wool shirt I had given him for Christmas last year. Red, brighter than the dull red of my darling's blood. At this moment, I was thankful to be a zhombie. There was no way I could tell the Sheriff that my husband had run right past me and off that cliff looking for me. I was grateful I could repeat my story, over and over and not have to feel it.

I found a room in a boarding house in Omak, near the county courthouse, to use as a base until the police would let me leave.

I drove our truck home through the pouring rain every step of the way. I wasn't able to cry, so I thanked the sky for crying for me.

I pulled up in front of our neat little house. The horses blinked at me across the fence. They had full hayracks, so our farm sitter was doing a good job. Two cat heads popped up in the window. Then three. Then four. I rested my head on the steering wheel for a minute. Finally, I gathered myself and opened the truck door. I had to go tell our little "family" their Dad was gone.

Then I had to find out how to get the one who did it.

Because I knew who killed Fleming, you bet I did. SoulJumper was probably aware the instant we crossed the Okanogan county line. In hindsight, I don't see how I could have been so stupid as to think we could get away with it. Tooling right up to Tonasket in broad daylight and all. Of course SoulJumper knew we were there and why.

I wouldn't make that mistake again.

* * *

Life and non-life went on. SoulJumper gave me no more lucid moments like that day in the tepee when he told me he wasn't a zhombie. Realizing I had questions to ask, he made sure I never got the chance. I was either in my life, isolated from everything zhombie, or I was under his control. Maintaining the façade of humanity kept me busy. I bought a couple of pigs to feed the groceries I never ate. Working, making house payments, fixing fences – all of it kept my mind off the loneliness. I had realized I would have to face the fact of Fleming's death. Just not so soon.

I spent a lot of time in the living room by the fire. Fleming's chair sat there, screaming with emptiness. Trying hard not to look at it, I would focus on the flames. Before long, I could pretend to go to bed. Lights out at ten, like always. One last walkabout, then to bed, where I never slept anymore.

Sometimes I got up and wandered around. I figured I could get away with a certain amount of eccentricity. Mostly, I laid there, watching the darkness change. I made myself keep breathing because I didn't want to get out of the breathing habit, so I'd count breaths and wait for my control time to start.

At last my mind began to clear.

I vowed to teach myself to sharpen my attention during control times, something I'd been unwilling to do before. Instead of being the dreamed, I wanted to be the dreamer. I made a point of doing one small something out of the character of my control being, with every trick, in every world.

The control of a zhombie is "scripted" as it were, by the master. I had been taught I could not do anything SoulJumper did not intend. I started testing boundaries, beginning with teaching myself to reach out and move an item. A book, a candle, a vase, whatever. Even such an insignificant act was a struggle. My arms refused to move. Then the john would touch me and they would reach out. I was frustrated and getting very tired of sexual slavery. Then, one night, every emotion I could still feel crystallized into one – determination. Clear and clean, free of anger or pain, like a mountain wind laden with the smell of snow.

I lifted my arm!

The man across the table from me somewhere in the future looked up from the tiny computerized device implanted in the back of his hand. I must have looked like a drunken conductor; I had no control; my arm sailed up and down and around. Inside, I was laughing and crying all at once. "Woohoo! I *did* it!" Luckily, I didn't have the ability to show my exultation on my face. I put my arm down and smiled seductively. The john bared his teeth at me and went back to his device. I don't think this guy's Mom would let him have a computer when he was a kid. He sure was paying a lot of money to ignore me.

I couldn't have been more pleased.

It took more than one control time but I managed to stick with it. I felt like I was in in control of something, anyway, no matter how small.

Sitting by my lonely fire one night in February, I realized I had another power.

I could call SoulJumper to me.

Chapter Ten

I got up and went into the kitchen, turning on every light on the way. I didn't want SoulJumper showing up and sitting in Fleming's chair. Standing next to the counter, I said, "Winston Two-Feathers."

Nothing.

Try again, with *feeling*. He wanted to appear last time. He wouldn't be so willing now. I straightened my shoulders and centered all my energy on one thought.

"WINSTON TWO-FEATHERS!"

I was prepared and still he startled me. He didn't look very happy.

"Who taught you that?"

I moved some things around on the counter hoping he wouldn't notice he had scared me.

SoulJumper laughed and said, "Freaked yourself out, did you?" He sobered. "Who taught you that?"

"You did."

We had a staring contest for a couple of minutes. SoulJumper looked away first. "Okay, so you're not stupid. What do you want?"

"I want answers. I want to know how to un-make myself."

"Is that why you went looking for Sharon?"

I went and sat at the kitchen table. On Fleming's side. I couldn't think of that trip without feeling hollow. "Yes."

SoulJumper sat across from me. "You're way off base. But if you want to see her, I'll tell you where she is."

This was too easy. There had to be a catch. I said as much to SoulJumper.

"No catch. You're just not going to get anywhere."

Oh, he was *so* sure of himself! I wanted to wipe that smug expression off his face. Preferably with a cast iron frying pan. "Does she still live in Tonasket with her grandmother?"

SoulJumper got a good laugh from that. He laughed and gasped, slapping the table with his right hand like punctuation. *What* was so all-fired funny?

"You go find Sharon. You won't have far to go. She moved to Big Sur last year."

No wonder SoulJumper got such a big kick out of the situation. We never had to go to Tonasket. All we had to do was drive twenty-five miles south on Highway 1. No cabin, no Lifetaker.

"Why did you kill Fleming?"

SoulJumper stood up, hiked his pants and shot his cuffs. "I didn't. You did. You called him into another dimension and he went."

I stared at SoulJumper, aghast.

He stared back, eyes cold and dead. "I sent you through time and made you scream like you'd been hurt. Then you ran ahead and led him off that cliff. You did it, Lisa."

My soul writhed. I couldn't have cared what SoulJumper did at this point. This was the ultimate evil.

SoulJumper leaned close. I imagined flames licking his lips as he spoke.

"Sharon McCall."

He was gone and I was alone with myself.

* * *

I sat in misery without moving for what must have been several hours. When I did look at the clock, it was almost my control time. Anger surged in me. I was *sick* of control times!

Anger was easier to bear than agony.

Guilty. Guilty as charged and I didn't even know I was doing it. Didn't even remember…hold it. That's right. I didn't remember leading Fleming off Lifetaker and I should.

I racked my brain. Nothing. Not a wisp.

That *liar!* I knew SoulJumper was disgusting but this was way beyond anything I could imagine. How could he dream of making me believe I had lured Fleming off that cliff? I thought furiously. He was very certain. There was a ring of truth in his voice. My memories of everything I did under control were clear, though. Too clear. Painfully so.

Suddenly, I was in a brothel in New Orleans and a private home in San Francisco. It appeared to be current times. I was being dressed in familiar styles by a madam in New Orleans and a queen in San Francisco. The queen had better taste. The brothel had johns lined up; the private home appeared to be hosting a party. I was led to sitting rooms in both worlds to wait. Far away, the part of me that still had some connection with humanity raged.

I looked at a shot glass on a table in New Orleans and a cup on a coffee table in San Francisco. I reached out slowly, deliberately with my right arm; silk and lace clad picking up the cup, nylon covering the hand that grasped the shot glass. Evenly, keeping my mind focused in both realities, I lifted the shot glass and cup to my lips. I looked over both brims and caught a pair of intensely green eyes staring at me.

In both worlds. Same eyes.

I froze.

Our gazes locked. I could hear distant chatter in the brothel. The johns were coming in. Soon the party would begin in San Francisco as well. Still, we sat without moving, neither of us even breathing.

She wasn't breathing!

She was a zhombie, too.

Seemingly in slow motion, in two worlds at once, she moved elegant arms and mimicked my action. Exactly. Without removing her gaze from mine, she picked up a shot glass and cup, lifted them to her lips. I was too frightened to think. My first reaction was that she had been planted by

SoulJumper to spy on me. I couldn't let him discover my new-found power!

Red-gold hair framing her face like an aura, she looked like an angel. Curls tumbled down her back to her waist. She was dressed in white in both worlds – probably to accentuate her angelic quality. Slender and tall, she looked too perfect to be real. Still, we stared. I heard door chimes in San Francisco and the madam's voice outside the door in New Orleans. In both worlds, the angel's lips moved.

"I'm Barbara," she whispered.

Doors flew open and guests streamed in; Southern accents sibilant, Western ones more flattened and nasal. Laughter, glass clinking and ribald conversations grew louder in both worlds.

The only thing I heard was, "I'm Barbara."

Chapter Eleven

That night, I went through the motions even more robotically than usual. The San Francisco party was a bunch of frat boys. In the brothel, I was usually in a room with a john. I kept seeing those green eyes and that graceful arm aping the clumsy motion of my own. I felt I had to find some way to communicate before my control time was up or I'd lose her forever. It was obvious she had more power than I because she could speak. As the minutes ticked by, I began to chafe. Frat boys were passing out and johns were going home to their wives.

Incredibly, I heard a short, fat man with an Alabama twang ask Barbara her name. Would she use a pseudonym? That was the stock response; a suggestive alias. In San Francisco, she was exiting a room with a boy who didn't look old enough to be in college. In both worlds, she glanced at me.

"Barbara Sheridan of the Slidell Sheridans."

Slidell, Louisiana. Just across Lake Ponchartrain from New Orleans, I discovered later when I looked it up in my trusty atlas. Home again, I sat at the kitchen table with Louisiana spread before me. I looked up Slidell's area code in the phone book and called information for the listing for Barbara Sheridan. I almost dropped the phone when the computer voice recited the number at me. Ma Bell was repeating it when I managed to write it down with shaking fingers.

Now what?

It was nearly 7A.M. in California, close to 9 in Louisiana. I wondered about Barbara's control times. They had to be almost identical to mine because she showed up shortly after me and was still there when I dematerialized. I could see her through the changing room door that had been left open. We didn't manage eye contact again but I sensed the next move was up to me.

I picked up the phone and started to dial.

* * *

After three rings, she answered. "Hello?"

I said stupidly, "Barbara?" cleared my throat and tried again. "Barbara, I'm Lisa."

"Lisa of New Orleans and San Francisco?"

"Yes."

"I was hoping you would call! When are your control times? Two to six?"

Nonplussed, I answered, "1:56 to 5:56."

Barbara said, "Good. Mine are 2:14 to 6:14. Where do you live?"

This conversation wasn't going as I planned. Why was I the only one answering questions? "How did you learn to speak during your control time?"

"I did the same thing you're doing. I started with tiny movements and worked up to more difficult ones." She sighed. "I understand you're nervous. Look at it this way. You know where I live."

She had a point there.

"I want to come visit you. Is that possible?"

I sat for a second weighing the dangers in one hand and opportunities in the other.

"Lisa, you there?"

"I'm Lisa Hutchinson Blakely Fleming and I live in Carmel Valley, California."

"Good. I'll call you when I've got travel plans. I should know something today."

Barbara hung up and I listened to the dial tone until a voice in the phone told me that if I wanted to make a call,

please hang up and dial again.
   What had I done?

Chapter Twelve

I turned on the answering machine and drove in the old truck to Big Sur. No telling when I might need four-wheel drive down there. If I got off the main roads, the side roads were a mess in winter. I couldn't just sit at the house and wait for the phone to ring. For a zhombie, I was a nervous wreck.

I kept telling myself not to worry. It wasn't helping. I wished I could enjoy a piece of chocolate. Munching chocolate had gotten me through many an emotional turmoil in my life and I missed it. No sense in it when it's tasteless and there are no endorphins for it to activate. I felt like I was on overload.

The ocean and dramatic coastline held no solace for me this morning. Gunmetal gray, they chilled me. I snuggled, unnecessarily, deeper into my down coat. No down coat in the world would do anything for the cold I felt.

I went back to Fleming's death, searching again for any memory of calling to Fleming, then running ahead of him. It was useless. The only memory I had was of running behind him, calling frantically for him to stop. I wanted desperately to disbelieve but I couldn't. I had a sinking feeling SoulJumper was telling the truth.

My mind churning, I drove through most of the town of Big Sur before I realized it. As it was, there were only a couple of resorts left before I was out on open highway. I pulled into a restaurant/bar/store and campground. Tucked under the redwoods, it hardly ever saw the sun. I loved the big trees but I could never live in them because they always made me feel like a mushroom. This place fit my mood; cheap and tawdry, with an underlying air of menace. One of the least expensive resorts on the coast, tourists still gave it a wide berth. Locals with bad habits and bad secrets came here.

Good place to start looking for Sharon.

I walked into the bar. It smelled of years of spilled alcohol and lackadaisical cleaning crews. There was no one behind the bar, so I walked through the connecting door to the store. A dark haired woman, bone thin and closely resembling a vampire stood behind the counter watching a couple of boys trying to shoplift. She ignored me so completely, I thought maybe I had gone invisible. For a wild moment, I considered reaching across the counter and grabbing that skanky woman by the throat. She saved herself by acknowledging my existence. Eyes without a spark of interest in them slithered to me.

"Help you?"

Every weirdo in the world seems to turn up at some time in Big Sur. This woman was taking the cake, though. Fleming would have called her a skinny nappy vampire woman. He would have made me laugh and dispelled the eerie feeling that was coming over me. The thought warmed my cockles and galvanized me. "I'm looking for a woman named Sharon McCall. You wouldn't happen to know her, would you?"

The woman's eyes, black as nothingness had gone back to the two boys. "Put that back."

The boys and I all gaped at her.

"Take that box of cookies out of your jacket and put it back on the shelf."

The woman's voice raised the hackles on the back of my neck. From the looks of it, she had the complete attention of the boys, too. She sounded the way I would imagine Medusa sounded when she spoke. Her eyes had apparently turned the boys to stone.

The biggest one grabbed a box of cookies from his coat. Throwing them on the floor, he dashed out, the smaller boy on his heels.

The woman behind the counter sighed, walked over, picked up the cookies and put them back on the shelf. "Somebody will be complaining about broken cookies later."

Suddenly, Vampire Woman no longer looked like a vampire, she just looked tired. She turned to me and shook her head. "Happens all the time. Kids looking for a thrill." She came back behind the counter and leaned on it, spreading her fingers on the coin mat. She seemed to like the texture. "Yeah, I know Sharon McCall. She used to work here. Quit last month. Don't know what she's up to now. I heard she had a cabin somewhere on Pico Blanco."

"Do you know if she has a phone?"

"Used to. Land line. Cells don't work at her place."

That was putting it mildly. Cells didn't work in the majority of Big Sur. "You got a phone book?"

She dragged a tattered directory from under the counter. "Pay phone's outside, to your left. Can't leave the phone books out there any more because people steal them. Some of these kids will steal anything that isn't nailed down but the tourists wanting a free souvenir are even worse."

I thanked my lucky stars I didn't work in Big Sur as I looked up the number and pushed the phone book across the counter. "Appreciate it."

"Come back when you can stay longer!" The woman flashed a smile and cackled. I reverted to thinking of her as Vampire Woman and went to find the phone.

* * *

The phone was next to the bathrooms, which stank of urine. Delightful. I wondered if anyone stayed long after smelling them. I didn't know what drew people to this place, didn't want to know. I did know it wasn't cleanliness. Or charm. The planters all had dead flowers. Yuck. I turned to the phone, dropped in two quarters and punched in Sharon's number.

"Hello."

"Sharon? This is…"

"You've reached the McCall ranch. Please leave your name and number at the beep."

I *hated* people who did that! I wondered how many partial messages she got because of one dumb joke. "Sharon, this is Lisa. Please call me." And I left my number. She'd know who I was.

I went back to my truck and sat for a minute, thinking. Vampire Woman came out of the store, squinted at the daylight and began to sweep. Here I was calling her names and she was probably a lot more normal than I was! She looked up, caught me staring, smiled and waved. Embarrassed, I waved back and started the truck. Might as well head north. Nothing left to do here.

I drove slowly through Big Sur, trying not to think. Maybe if I just let things percolate, they would arrange themselves in some kind of order in my head.

When I got to the Old Coast Road, for some reason, I took it. The Old Coast Road is just that. Prior to Highway 1, the Old Coast Road meandered inland before paralleling the ocean. February is not the best time of year for it; being unpaved, it's usually a sea of mud. The old timers knew their stuff, though. At least big chunks of the Old Coast Road didn't fall off in the ocean every year.

I stopped to lock the hubs and looked back at the Pacific. The clouds had broken up in spots and shafts of golden sunlight appeared to pierce the ocean. A whale spouted, then another and another. "That's right," I thought, "The whales are running." I felt mildly ecstatic.

That was the first thing that penetrated my shell. Grief is a terrible thing when you can't cry. The whales seemed to call to me, "We understand. We feel your pain. We have broad backs, huge hearts. Let us carry it for you."

Fancy? Maybe. Delusion? Who cares?

Those whales pierced the muck that was surrounding me as surely as the rays of sun pierced the clouds. I stood there with the wind blowing in my face and felt beauty touch me for the first time in many months. Maybe there was hope for me after all.

* * *

The rude honking of a horn jerked me out of my reverie. So much for blissful moments. Even here in Big Sur, the last bastion of the sixties, you had road rage. I turned, scowling at the green SUV nose to nose with my truck. The driver's window sighed down. Out popped a brassy blonde head. Smacking gum as fast as she talked, Sharon said, "I heard you were looking for me."

Why was I not surprised? Big Sur was practically incestuous. Everyone knew everyone. Vampire Woman had probably called her the instant my shadow had cleared the door. "Don't know what she's up to," indeed. Sharon seemed amused. I hadn't said a word and I'm sure she enjoyed having me at a disadvantage.

"Want to follow me to my place? It's not far and the road's good."

I *had* come to find her, so I may as well go. "Sure."

"Let me get turned around."

She told the truth, her place was only a couple of miles in, with only one spot where I was mudding. We pulled up at a cedar shake cabin next to the Little Sur River. The day was clearing and sunshine filtered through the redwoods, sparkling on the river. Shamrocks grew in profusion under the trees. Sharon had put a bathtub out over the river. Oooh, that would be heavenly. I wondered if bathing soothed her, too. A path wandered under the Redwood trees, headed upriver. A small water wheel turned, shushshushshush.

Sharon slammed the door of her SUV and said, "Come on in. I'll make us some tea."

"No thanks."

Sharon stopped and looked at me quizzically.

"I know it's like shutting the barn door after the horses get out but I'm not drinking anymore tea with you. Ever."

Sharon burst out laughing. "It's always best to be careful. Come on in. I won't bite and I won't offer you tea."

"If you don't mind, I'd rather stay out here." Obstinately.

"Suit yourself." Sharon shrugged. "You should know better by now, though."

Know better? What did she mean by that? I thought for a second. "You mean because there's no protection?"

"Not once you've been chosen."

Sharon disappeared into the cabin and returned carrying two expensive camp chairs. The kind you order from a catalogue and never take camping because they're too nice. Hers were black and comfortable. We sat facing the river.

"Who chose me?"

Sharon stretched out a foot and looked it over. "I did."

I didn't understand. I said out loud. "I thought SoulJumper…"

"SoulJumper? Is that your name for Winston?"

Drat. Now she would tell him and the name would be useless. I looked at Sharon and mumbled, "Yes."

"Good one. It suits him." She leaned back, cradling her head in the chair and looked up at the redwoods. "I'm only going to tell you this once. You will never be free. You belong to me and I will never let you go."

* * *

I couldn't think of anything to say. Now that she had dropped her bombshell, Sharon sat examining her manicure. So everyday and normal, it made what she had said seem even more freakish. I couldn't match the woman with the statement.

"Ah…Winston…" I sounded like a strangled chicken. Why couldn't I ever be dignified under pressure?

"Winston is a very accomplished sorcerer. I pay him extremely well."

This was all so...so! I was having trouble making the pieces fit. I think I even shook my head to clear it.

"If you don't want to drive home after your control time tonight, you'd better get going."

I stirred. She was right. Each time I dematerialized from this world, I left an image. A memory of an image is more like it. Somewhat like a photographic negative. My physical self returned to that by threads of thought. If I stayed at Sharon's, I would be stuck driving Highway 1 at night. Twenty-some-odd miles of twists, turns, cliffs and fog. There are so many accidents on that road, emergency room staff at a local hospital had a "West on One" club. You go West on One, you don't come back.

I had one more question. Well, maybe two. "Are you a zhombie?"

"I am."

"Do you have control times?"

Sharon turned to look at me and suddenly the wind began to whip in the tops of the trees. Clouds scudded across the sun, giving the light a strobe effect. Sharon seemed to grow and shrink, grow and shrink. All the light in the day centered on her head. *Her hair was forming into snakes!*

As quickly as the image began, it was gone. The wind died, sunlight trickled through the trees, the water wheel went shushshushshush. Sharon's hair was nothing but overbleached blonde hair. She smacked her gum at me and reached for a pack of cigarettes in the pocket of her chair. She puffed a cloud of smoke around her head, mocking me.

I sat frozen, not wanting to comprehend.

Sharon nudged me with her toe. "Y'all come back now, y'hear?"

Her Southern accent stank!

Chapter Thirteen

Driving home, a storm blew in from the ocean and the rain slanted across my windshield. I was thankful I hadn't stayed. The weather didn't look to be clearing any time soon. From the size of the cloudbank over the ocean, this one could set up housekeeping for a few days.

I was paying attention to the weather so I wouldn't have to think. Instead of facing facts, I played little games. When a mental picture of Sharon with snakes in her hair did filter in, I diverted myself. What was it with me and Medusa all of a sudden? I had seen her in Vampire Woman and Sharon in the space of one morning.

Of course. I had called that image to me because she was in my mind. Sharon didn't create Medusa, I did. All Sharon did was supply the energy. I did all the visualizing myself. I felt something shift inside me with a satisfying "chink". Solidification of will. I love it. One more board in my freedom chest. Since reality is an illusion and we all create our own, I wondered how much of my bondage was created by me. As long as I believed in it, it was real.

I couldn't *wait* to talk to Barbara!

I got back to the farm just in time to throw some hay to the horses, fill the pigs' trough and take care of the cats. I always like to make sure all the animals have food and water before my control times, now I'm alone. I noticed the answering machine light blinking but I figured that could wait.

I was scooping the cats' litter box when I dematerialized. Actually, I had just finished and was hanging the plastic scoop back on its hook. For some reason, the scoop went with me! I showed up at a palace in ancient China, grasping a plastic poop scoop.

Normally, when I arrive in other worlds, it's a cloistered event. Zhombies received me and dressed me. No one else saw me until I was attired for the period. This time, exactly at the moment I was materializing, the chamber door slid open and a man walked in. A servant, bringing water. The poor guy's eyes practically popped out of his head. No telling what he thought. Here I appeared out of thin air wearing jeans, sweatshirt and boots, waving that ridiculous poop scoop.

He fainted. Water splashed everywhere. In my mind, I'm laughing so hard, if I hadn't been a zhombie under control, I would have fallen down. I finally managed to think, "Winston Two-Feathers!" SoulJumper (I did like that name for him) appeared and got a gander at me standing there like some freakazoid Statue of Liberty. Then looked at the manservant passed out cold in a pool of water by the door. He was not amused. I swear, that man had absolutely no sense of humor.

He whisked me home where I finished hanging up the poop scoop. Then I laughed so hard, I had to grab onto a chair.

That's when I noticed SoulJumper fading in and out.

I stopped laughing, curious; snorted a couple of tee-hees and rubbed my eyes. Nope. He was solid. But for a second there, I could have sworn he was a victim of bad reception.

Winston jerked me out of there and tossed me into a tent in Roman times. Great. I was a camp follower. As the "zhombettes" washed and dressed me, my mind was going a million miles an hour. I wondered if I had imagined the flickering Two-Feathers incident and decided I had not. I replayed it over and over in my mind.

Now I definitely couldn't wait to talk to Barbara!

* * *

I played my messages as soon as I got home. Barbara had called at 10:35 A.M. with flight plans. She would be arriving in Monterey on the 9 A.M. flight tomorrow morning. She would rent a car, then call me for directions. I glanced at the clock. Her control time wasn't up for another fifteen minutes; no sense in trying to call her yet.

Now what? Here I was, all dressed up, as it were, and no place to go! On fire to talk to someone. *Man,* I missed Fleming! I decided to talk to him anyway. At the very least, his chair. As the rain poured on the roof, I built a fire and got myself situated. One of the cats – Lugnut – curled up on my lap. His name was apropos. He purred and kneaded the air with gray paws.

I wasn't sure how to begin. I shifted, momentarily disturbing Lugnut. He blinked accusingly at me and redistributed himself. I felt distinctly like an idiot. Not exactly a novel sensation for me, so I plunged ahead.

"Fleming," I began, "I miss you" and it all came pouring out. How sad I was without him and I merely existed on the surface since his death. I finally babbled my way around to Two-Feathers' story; that I'd lured Fleming off LifeTaker. Everything that I had left in me cried out in anguish. Anguish borne alone and unreleased. I talked and talked, saying silly nothings like the horses had thicker coats this year and did he think it was time to trim the tree in the big pasture? Staring at the fire, I imagined Fleming stretching in his chair and smiling at me.

Oh, this was awful. This was a very, very bad idea. Every ounce of my being wanted Fleming there with me.

Then I looked at his chair and he *was!*

I blinked.

He was still there. Hazy but there, indeed.

He looked me in the eye and said clearly, "I need to talk to you," and was gone.

Okay, I was starting to feel like one of those boxing clowns. The ones with the rounded bottoms and when you hit them, they bob back up at you. This was way too much input for one day.

I drew myself a bath.

When Fleming was alive, I told him it soothed me to bathe. So he made a beautiful redwood surround tub for me and set it in a greenhouse full of flowers. The tub was oversized, lined with stone and kidney shaped so Fleming and I could face each other and soak.

Leaning back in the water, I tried to let my mind drift. Easier said than done. I concentrated on feeling the water against my skin. I couldn't feel the temperature but I could feel the fact of the water; the pressure on my body. Still enjoyable, even without the sensation of warmth.

Orchids and ginger were blooming. They both looked as though they could use a drink. When I emptied the tub, I would divert the water to the drip system in the greenhouse rather than outside. It was still raining and the ground was saturated anyway.

I was wasting time and I desperately needed it. I simply had to keep everything at bay for a little while. Barbara would be here soon enough and I could deal with everything then.

I frittered away the entire evening until my control time, doing girly things. Ironing clothes, straightening pillows, brushing my hair, looking through my closet for clothes I could give to charity, making room for new ones.

I made sure when 1:56 rolled around, I wasn't holding anything in my hand.

Chapter Fourteen

I was off to two worlds in the future this time. In one, I was not allowed to wear clothes. Dressed only in a homing device strapped around my throat, I was led onto a stage and auctioned off. The man who bought me paid with small platinum bars. Worth a fortune in my time, probably about a hundred dollars in his. After all, I was forty-nine years old. He took me to his house and showed me my room. He was kind of sweet, disregarding the fact that he believed people could be bought and sold. I knew that he didn't have a clue that I would dematerialize in about an hour's time, never to be seen again. SoulJumper was expanding into new markets.

The other world was more what I was accustomed to – someone needed mothering. People were androgynous to look at but I was pretty sure the client was female. I never did find out for certain because he/she never undressed.

I was relieved to get back to my little house. Only three hours until Barbara's flight arrived.

I mucked out stalls and threw the horses some hay. I fed the pigs and thought that it was time to go to the grocery store. More food I wouldn't eat.

At 8:30, I went inside, washed the horse dirt off my hands and sat in the kitchen waiting for the phone to ring. I thought about making coffee, just to have something to do with my hands but decided against it. I was too lazy to clean up the mess afterward. At long last – the watched pot syndrome – the phone rang. I picked it up on the second ring. "Hello?"

"Hi, Lisa, it's Barbara. I'm at the airport and I've rented a car. How do I get to you?"

I wasn't all that far from the airport and within twenty minutes a navy blue economy car pulled in my drive. I could see the cloud of golden red hair from where I stood. Waving her to a place to park, I smiled in welcome.

She got out, stretched with one hand in the small of her back. She looked around her, turning slowly, taking it all in. She faced me, green eyes pinning me to the ground. "So how do you deal with your memories?"

This woman *never* said what you expected! She did, however, go right to the heart of a matter with no hesitation. No frittering or dancing around the truth for this one. She faced facts squarely, examining everything under the spotlights of those green eyes. Maybe she could teach me a thing or two. "It's not easy. Won't you come in?"

We grabbed Barbara's luggage and walked to the house. She traveled light; garment bag and overnight case.

"It can't be easy, coming back to all this beauty twice a day."

"It's not," I said. "Is it for you? What's your life like?"

Barbara sighed. "All paneled walls and colonial mansions that look like Tara. I was supposed to marry a Southern gentleman, live in Slidell and raise a lot of children who never speak until they're spoken to and say yes sir and yes ma'am." She looked sad. "I was perfectly suited for the life and would have enjoyed children and grandchildren immensely."

"How old were you when you were taken?"

"I was eighteen."

"Who made you?"

By this time, we had reached the front door. Barbara smiled at me and said, "Why don't we go inside and sit down. I'll tell you all about me."

I liked this woman but she really had a talent for making me feel gauche! Flustered, I opened the door and motioned her in. "Would you like a cup of coffee?"

"That would be delightful."

Whoever Barbara Sheridan was, she was a lady.

* * *

We sat at the kitchen table, steaming mugs in front of us. She took hers black, which was a good thing, since I had given the last of the milk to the pigs. I stirred a little sugar into mine so I wouldn't be sitting there doing nothing. Barbara didn't have the same qualms. She did nothing very well. Completely at ease, she seemed totally unconcerned that the conversation had come to a screeching halt. Just when I was getting ready to say something – anything – to break the silence, Barbara said, "I'm two hundred years old."

"Gee, you don't look a day of it."

Barbara laughed. "I'm glad you have a sense of humor. You're going to need it." She crossed elegant legs. "I haven't lived two hundred years in this time. I was taken from my time and brought to this one. My family think I disappeared, probably eaten by an alligator. Of course, no trace was ever found.

I live in Slidell in a two-story Victorian house. I am watched over and cared for by an elderly woman who gets paid well for her trouble. She knows enough that I don't have to hide too much from her but not everything. She thinks that I am a very high-class prostitute and takes pride in grooming me. She was chosen for her lack of intelligence.

I have been a zhombie for about ten years now. For the last five, I have been working to find a way to free myself." Barbara stared into space for a moment, then took a tiny sip of coffee. "When I saw you in San Francisco and New Orleans doing the same things I had done, I knew you were trying to free yourself, too."

"Scared me to death when I caught you watching me. I thought SoulJumper had sent you to spy on me."

"SoulJumper?" Barbara took another infinitesimal sip. I bet she cut her food in itty-bitty pieces, too. I'd never felt so unfeminine!

"My name for Winston. You know, Mr. Two-Feathers." I shrugged.

"Yes." Barbara's eyes hardened. By now I could have been chipping ice out of them. "Mr. Two-Feathers."

"That's who made me," I said.

"And me, as well. He'll be the first one I destroy."

Woo! And I thought *I* was angry! "Is there a way? To destroy him, I mean? I know he's not a zhombie, is he immortal?"

About as immortal as you can get and still be human." Barbara said flatly. "They say the good die young and he's living proof."

I snickered. She had a pretty good sense of humor herself. Barbara took another tiny sip. I had a vision of a huge dining room and a voice saying, "Ladies don't eat like field hands."

"First and foremost, we can't let anyone know we're together," Barbara said. "I've managed to gather some information through the years and I know the powers that be don't like us joining forces."

"So you don't like using his name, either?" I bet *she* didn't almost wet her pants the first time he appeared!

Barbara gave a little giggle. "The first time he showed up out of nowhere, I almost peed my pants! I vowed I would never do that again!"

Maybe she wasn't perfect after all. Jealousy wasn't going to get me anywhere. I was acting like an adolescent. I giggled and said, "Same here." Our eyes met in laughter – girls will be girls. It was a bonding moment.

From that time on, I was sure I could trust Barbara. We were in this together, in more ways than one. Two women, lives controlled and ruined by one man, with an eternity to live with the damage. Two women with one thought…to destroy one man.

* * *

Barbara and I toasted each other with our coffee mugs. She glanced at a tiny diamond watch draped around her wrist.

How in the world did she manage to read the thing? Oh, that's right. She was only eighteen. I had another brief pang of envy. She got to be eighteen forever. Barbara's voice brought me back to my senses. "It's only a quarter to eleven. Good. We've got time to talk."

We settled into our chairs. I don't know what it is but I love to hang out in the kitchen. In the good old days, if I had women friends over, that's where we ended up. Drinking coffee and yakking. Evidently Barbara liked kitchens, too. We were going to get along just fine.

Barbara nailed me with those eyes again. "I'm your great-great- grandmother. If we don't get me back to my time line, I'm not sure what will happen in yours."

I froze with my coffee cup halfway to my lips. A cat meowed.

"Are you okay?"

I set my mug down with a thud. "You like to go right for the jugular, don't you?"

Barbara raised an eyebrow at me. "Don't you think you're being a tad dramatic?"

Dramatic. I had known nothing about my family, really. My grandmother had a dispute with her Father and left some nebulous part of the East, came to California and married a minister. Episcopalian. She had two kids and never told them anything about her history. I had an uncle who had gone to Ellis Island to research us and had come up with nothing. Dramatic? Okay, if I was, I think I had the right! I calmed myself. "There are several things you'll need to explain to me."

Barbara smiled. "That's my girl."

I stuck out my tongue at her. Now she sounded like a great-great-grandmother and I was acting like a two-year old. This was so much *better*. "Why am I here at all if you weren't in your time to give birth to whatever ancestor it is that leads to me?"

"Because when your DNA was taken, you were frozen in time, that very night. You entered an alternate reality before you ever left that tepee."

"And?"

"I was taken and made, immediately after you were chosen." Barbara got up and paced the kitchen. "They know their stuff, the ones who are doing this. They've been at it for hundreds of years. They need the maternal line and don't want to wait for the babies to be born anymore. All of us; you, me, Anna, Rachel, Cynthia, Louise and Natalie are related through the women's line. That way, the power is intact."

"There are *seven* of us?" I paused to digest this. "What about Sharon? That would make it eight."

Barbara turned from her pacing. "Sharon is the one behind it all."

Actually, this wasn't news to me. I told Barbara about the visit and Medusa stunt.

"That sounds like her. She loves display." Barbara came and sat again. In my old chair. I was in Fleming's. I still wasn't up to seeing anyone else sit there.

"So what you're telling me is that all of us are related and Sharon is actually in charge and not a zhombie." I took a deep breath. "She told me she was."

Barbara was already nodding. "She is. She freed herself from her creator, somehow, long ago. He was the one who started the prostitution on a lesser scale. His world only, no time travel or dual realities. That's all Sharon's doing. I'm not sure how or when she met the Two-Feathers rat. I only know he's old too. He never was a zhombie. He is a sorcerer from someplace in Spain who has perfected the art of living off the energy of humans. A ghoul. His primary targets are the dying and infants. He sucks their life force like smoke out of them. It's disgusting."

We were silent, busy with our individual thoughts about SoulJumper. I thought how accurate the name was now. "What do we do?"

Barbara grinned wickedly. "We find us a way to skin a ghoul."

* * *

I snapped to attention, staring at Barbara across what suddenly was miles of kitchen table. "You said wait for the babies to be born. Was I supposed to have a baby?"

Barbara looked back, her eyes emerald pools of understanding. "As far as I can deduce, yes. I haven't been to that reality but I think we can safely say you would have had a little girl. Have you married?"

I nodded. I couldn't think of a thing to say.

Barbara put a hand over mine. "And your husband is…?"

"Dead. Fleming's dead. He killed him but he said I did it." I was getting overrun with "he's" but I didn't care. "He said he made me run ahead and call him off LifeTaker but I don't remember. I swear, Barbara, I don't!"

Barbara squatted in front of me, taking my hands in hers. "Wait, honey, slow down. You're getting all jumbled up. Are you breathing?"

I inhaled. "I wasn't but I am now."

"Good." Barbara smiled into my eyes, squeezed my hands and stood. She sat across the table from me and checked her watch. Smiling serenely, she said, "Tell me what happened."

I had to get this woman back to her own time if for nothing else than the fact that she was going to make a fantastic mother. She was one of the more comforting people I had ever met. It felt odd to be mothered by an eighteen year old. I reminded myself that not only was she not eighteen but she had witnessed things the majority of humanity never sees and been to worlds they weren't aware existed.

I told her. It felt wonderful to get it all out. I had never told anyone the whole truth. I couldn't. They'd never believe me. I could tell Barbara about Fleming running by, unseeing, and myself running after calling, desperately calling, almost going off LifeTaker after him and how I wished I could have. I took a breath. "That's why when SoulJumper told me I led Fleming off that cliff, I couldn't understand. I have no memory of it."

"That's because SoulJumper, as you call him, went into an alternate reality and took a *you* that never married. He used the alternate Lisa, not the real one."

"At this point, I'm starting to wonder which is the real Lisa?"

Barbara flipped a curl out of her eye and pinned me again. Forest green and alive the light that washed over me from those incredible eyes. Why didn't I inherit those?

"*You* are, my dear. The consciousness that is aware right here, right now, is you. There are many parts to that consciousness but you are the central one."

"If we get this all straightened out; you back to your time line and me to mine; you get your life back and I get Fleming and a little girl?"

Barbara chuckled. "That's putting it simply but I think so." She folded her hands. I had never seen anyone actually fold their hands before. The way she did it, it had all the grace of a bygone era. "The trouble is, if we don't get us both back, those time lines are altered and die out for us. The longer we exist as zhombies, the less our human past exists. It finally fades altogether and we are left. Creatures of nothing and no one. No past, just an endless future of wandering to hide what we are." Barbara shook her head. "I don't intend to let that happen to either of us." She straightened her shoulders and slapped her palms on the table with a bright smile. "Well! It's almost control time. Shall we go get ready?"

I grinned impishly. "Sure, Granny."

That drew a snort from Barbara.

"What do we do if we bump into each other?" I asked.

"We never let 'em see us sweat."

We locked arms and went out of the kitchen giggling. "That'll be easy cuz we don't sweat."

Barbara elbowed me in the ribs. "No, darlin' we glow."

Laughing like teenagers we got Barbara settled into the spare room. We parted to prepare for control time in our separate ways; she to rest and me to check my animals. I actually sang under my breath. Surprised me, when I caught myself. It felt good.

Chapter Fifteen

I didn't run into Barbara but I did run into Anna. I was in current day New York and future Nashville, Tennessee. Anna was in New York with me at a private home. I tried my best to make eye contact with her, to no avail. It would have been easier if she had been in both worlds with me. My control time was up before I had any success.

I checked on my little farm while I waited for Barbara. When she came out of the bedroom she asked, "Do you mind if I take a bath?"

"Not at all. Rough time?" I showed Barbara to the greenhouse tub, opening the door slowly to let the room have its full impact. Barbara gazed around raptly, her hands clasped in front of her like a little girl.

"Lisa, it's gorgeous! What a delightful idea!"

"Fleming's. When I told him I still liked to bathe, he made this for me."

Barbara didn't say anything. Those eyes drank in the beauty that almost matched their own. I stood beside her, letting her enjoy. "Thank you, Lisa, for sharing this. I *did* have a rough time."

I handed her an oversized towel and washcloth. "Soap's in the bottle next to the faucet. Peppermint. Shampoo and conditioner are there on the table. Everything's biodegradable because I water the greenhouse and garden when I empty the tub. Help yourself." I went to vacuum the living room and left Barbara to distance herself from her memories.

Half an hour later, she emerged in a cobalt blue bathrobe and hair wrapped in a towel.

"Better?"

"Yes, thank you. It helps to at least try to wash the ugliness away." Barbara pulled the towel off her head and shook out her hair.

"Barbara, is that natural curl?"

She sat cross-legged on the towel in front of the fireplace, pulled a comb out of her pocket and began to comb her hair. "Yes, I was born with it. Natural color, too."

"Dang, girl, you sure weren't beat with the ugly stick, were you? What happened to me?"

Barbara smirked at me through a curtain of hair. "I guess the blood got watered down by the time it got to you. There's the male line to consider, you know."

I laughed out loud. That made me think of the fading Two-Feathers incident. I told Barbara about it.

"Pretty interesting. A fact to keep."

I got tired of watching Barbara trying to dry her hair in front of a fireplace with no fire and got up. "Skootch over," I said, nudging her with my foot.

"What?" She skootched.

"I'm gonna build you a fire so you can dry that ridiculous amount of hair you have on your head. The way things are going, you'll look like a drowned rat come your control time."

"Jealous."

"You're absolutely right! You couldn't be more right! How does anybody get off being so beautiful?" We were laughing again. I was doing a lot of that these last few days.

"Genes."

We both stopped laughing. Fire built, I curled up in Fleming's chair. Barbara and I sat, mesmerized by the flames. "How did you find out about me, Barbara?"

She started combing again. "I had been pumping our friend SoulJumper for a while. If Southern women learn anything at their mother's knee, it's how to get information out of a man." She smiled. "Even one who's a ghoul. And if you know him at all, you know he likes to talk."

I grunted. "Yes. His loose lips have worked in my favor, too. He told me he wasn't a zhombie, then had a spasm because he did and sent me home before my control time was over."

"Sharon would kill him. She hates it when she doesn't get paid for every second of our control time." Barbara shifted and stretched her legs out in front of her. "Bear in mind that it took time but over the years, I got the essentials of their plan. They needed seven women, related by the maternal line to create a circle of power. I was number six. They had chosen you and they came and got me. It was easy enough for them; they traveled to the time before the break in the family, then traced back to me. They kept going until they found me because they wanted a woman of physical beauty."

I started to say something consoling and Barbara waved a hand at me. "It's okay. Anyway, I knew when they finally made you because SoulJumper was exultant. He had to brag to someone and I made sure that someone was me. That's when he told me I was your great-great-grandmother, only now that line wouldn't exist. In a very short amount of time, relatively, you and I wouldn't be, except as his slaves. Forever.

I knew the circle of power was important. If they could utilize it, so could we. But I guessed it would take all of us. You were the only one I had never seen in other worlds. Until the other night. Now you know pretty much everything I do."

I got up and poked at the fire. "No idea what we have to do to free ourselves?"

She shook her head. "None."

"What are the others like? *Oh!* I have seen Anna. Matter of fact, I was with her this last control."

Barbara sat up straight. "Did you try to contact her?"

"I tried to meet her eyes but never did."

Barbara relaxed again. "I don't know how strong she is. I've seen her a lot and I've never been able to reach her. Either she can't or she won't. Or she knows more than she's letting on."

"That's possible. What about the others?"

"Rachel looks to have been about twenty-five when she was taken. She is dark and exotic and from your time. I don't know where she lives, though.

Louise has brown hair, short and curly. She has dimples and a cute, tomboyish air. She looks like a little boy; she may have been sixteen when she was made. She appears to be from your time and lives in the Midwest.

Cynthia has huge brown eyes and a fragile air. I don't know much about her.

Natalie is tall and Nordic. May have Russian lineage. She is icy and untouchable and astoundingly beautiful."

I sighed. More so than you? I'm gonna develop a complex!"

Barbara laughed. "You'll be fine."

Easy for her to say! "Have you contacted any of the others?"

"I have. Natalie and Rachel."

She sure knew how to draw out a punch line! I reached over and poked her.

"Okay, okay. They seemed responsive."

* * *

Barbara went to get some clothes on and I sat in front of the fire going over everything she had told me. It began to rain and I leaned forward to look out the window. Was it morning or evening? My life was dictated by control times...natural rhythms of sleep and waking nonexistent now.

Barbara came back in the living room dressed in beige linen lounging pajamas and chocolate silk mules. Classy.

"Barbara, do you eat?"

"No." She shook her head, curls glinting in the firelight. "Not when I don't have to, really. I do at home so my housekeeper doesn't get suspicious."

"I buy groceries and feed them to my pigs."

"Do you?" Barbara sat in "my" chair. "That's a smart idea." She leaned back and wriggled into the comfort of the chair.

"Why do you think they went into the past to get you rather than to the future to get my daughter?"

"I don't know, Lisa. I thought about that. Everyone else appears to be the natural last of their line. If they went back and got me, they stopped yours, as well. They can't allow us to have daughters for some reason."

"Maybe our daughters would mess up their circle of power somehow."

"I know from things SoulJumper has told me that when they got to you and I, making us, they were trying something. Trying to circumvent the demands for the circle of power. Maybe we all have to be the last of our line. Your daughter wouldn't have been, so they interfered. I would imagine it's not easy to find seven women, all related maternally, all the natural last of their line."

"Hello, ladies."

Barbara and I almost jumped out of our skin. The voice came from the kitchen doorway. Barbara got out of the chair and we stood side by side in front of the flickering fire facing SoulJumper as he walked in the room. Barbara slipped her arm through mine. I glanced at her and straightened my shoulders. We stared at SoulJumper together as he settled himself in Fleming's chair. A frisson of anger stirred my nerve endings. How dare he?

"I stopped in Slidell for a visit and your housekeeper told me you were gone for a few days." SoulJumper stared at Barbara. "To California. I thought it odd that you suddenly had a desire to visit California and decided to investigate. It's a good thing I did."

Barbara and I stood silently.

SoulJumper leaned forward. "What's up?"

Barbara squeezed my arm ever so slightly and said, "You can't control us now or you would have."

That was taking the bull by the horns! I settled myself for trouble.

SoulJumper's eyes narrowed. He took a deep breath and leaned back in Fleming's chair, crossing his legs. "I see." He looked at us with no expression. "It seems we are at an impasse. What do you suggest we do?"

A voice in my brain was telling me something was wrong. The last time SoulJumper was so agreeable, he sent me to Sharon. He had something up his sleeve. Barbara had gone rigid. Then suddenly, she relaxed, released my arm and sat in my chair. She smiled and leaned toward SoulJumper as if she was settling in for a cozy chat. "I don't know, Winston. What do you suggest?"

He looked at her as if she'd bitten him. "Don't try that on me. I'm going to watch and wait."

Barbara beamed southern charm. "You don't perceive us as a problem?"

SoulJumper stood up. Not looking at either of us, he said, "No, I don't." Then he fixed us with a gaze that had an eternity of night times in it. "Because I'll destroy you before I set you free."

Barbara's expression never changed, she still looked like a hostess at a tea party except for her eyes. They went as deep as an ocean. "You'll have to, Winston."

He looked from one of us to the other. Nodded his head and was gone.

"That went well, don't you think?" Barbara crossed her ankles delicately and brushed imaginary dust from her lap.

I gaped at her in astonishment and started to laugh. She slanted an impish glance at me and laughed. We hooted and hollered, slapping our legs and snorting in a very unladylike manner. When we finally wound down to an occasional "Whooee" and "My goodness" we tried to figure out what to do. Barbara opened the conversation.

"We have to find the others now. As soon as possible."

"How do we when all we have is first names and no location? We're not going to be able to get anything out of SoulJumper now."

Barbara sighed. "You got any chocolate? I could sure use some chocolate."

I looked at her, surprised. "You can taste it?"

"It's more a memory of the taste. I loved chocolate and would go to the kitchens and beg a piece whenever I could."

"Must run in the family, then. I loved it, too. I was just wishing the other day I could enjoy it again."

"Does that mean you have some?"

"No but the store isn't far and we can talk while we drive. We have to hurry, though. It's getting close to Time."

Barbara gave a little skip. "We can take my car." She ran to throw on some jeans.

I wedged myself into the passenger seat with my knees in my teeth. "This seat go back any?"

Barbara looked at me imitating a pretzel and laughed. "It might go back a little. Give it a try, I'll help." We wiggled and squirmed and pushed, finally getting the seat to give an inch. Even with zhombie strength, we couldn't coax any more out of it. At length, I said, "The store's not far. If we don't quit dinking with this seat, we're going to rip it out of its runners."

"Two delicate flowers of womanhood such as ourselves?"

That started us giggling again. By some miracle, Barbara got us out of my driveway and onto Carmel Valley Road. We didn't sober up until I said, "Why do you think SoulJumper gave up so easily?"

Barbara turned on the blinker to enter the parking lot. "I don't know. I don't like it."

We pulled in a space and I decanted myself. "I don't either. Maybe we should stick together from now on."

"You thinking about moving Granny in with you?"

I chuckled. Don't you think it would be simpler? We could work on finding the others and present a united front." I grabbed a buggy and motioned Barbara through the door ahead of me. "I've got to pick up a little more than chocolate. Do we have time?"

Barbara checked her watch. "We should. I'll keep an eye on the time and let you know if it's getting late. How long do you need to prepare?"

I put some apples in a sack. The horses would love these. "About thirty minutes. I like to make sure everyone's got fresh food and water and the house is locked. Don't want to end up in ancient China with a poop scoop again." That got Barbara. I told her the story and she had to hang onto the buggy, she was laughing so hard. Now *she* had a sense of humor! Humor. That reminded me. As we picked out bread, I asked, "What does our mind set have to do with everything?"

"I'm not sure but it's worthy of research. I think their enslavement of us may depend in a large part on our 'agreeing' in a way."

We stood in the checkout line. The clock on the wall in front of us said we had almost an hour. "You know, I came to almost the same conclusion after the Medusa incident. Because she was in my mind, I made Medusa manifest. Because we believe in our slavery, it's real." I paid the cashier and we walked out into a moment of glorious sunshine between rainstorms.

Barbara turned her face up to the sun, eyes closed, then popped them open at me. "What happens if we disbelieve? If we start detaching ourselves bit by bit?"

"I don't get it."

Barbara led us to the car and I wadded myself back up in the passenger seat. Turning on the ignition, Barbara said, "What is the prevailing emotion you've felt since you were taken? Granted, emotion is different now but what would you say has been your most common frame of mind?"

I thought for a minute. "Sadness."

"Exactly. Mine as well. Maybe we feed the zhombie reality with our sadness. How long did it take you before that changed?"

"Months. Almost a year."

"What was the catalyst?"

"I don't know. One day control time was near and I got angry about it. I got tired of the whole idea...getting snatched out of my life twice a day into sexual slavery. I decided to pay closer attention during control times, something I'd been unwilling to do before."

"Same with me. I went from being a docile participant to an aware one. Is that when you started practicing picking things up?"

"Yeah. It took a while but that's when I started."

We turned into my drive and as we unloaded groceries, Barbara said, "I think they depend on our docility, our acceptance of the status quo."

I let us in the door and we went into the kitchen and started putting groceries away. At least, I did. As soon as Barbara found a chocolate bar, she pounced on it with a squeal of joy and sat at the kitchen table to eat. I closed a cupboard and said, "If that's true, why wasn't SoulJumper worried when he found us together?"

Barbara swallowed a teensy-weensy bite before answering. "I don't know. It's suspicious. He could have been bluffing."

I went back to SoulJumper's visit, replaying his every expression. "Didn't feel like a bluff to me." I grinned idiotically. "Maybe he's okay with it."

Barbara wrinkled her nose at me. "Okay or not, he's going to have to live with it."

I sat across from her. "Does that mean you're moving in?"

Barbara dotted her lips with a napkin. "It does, indeed."

Chapter Sixteen

We went our separate ways to prepare. This time I went to current day Florida and ancient England. I wore a housedress and slippers with curlers in my hair in Florida and a dress that bared my breasts in England. Once attired, I was led to a sitting room in England and a kitchen in Florida. In both worlds, I was left to wait. I focused my attention on my right arm, getting ready to pick up a saltshaker and a china cherub. Doors opened, simultaneously, in two worlds. My chance was lost for now. I felt my mind slipping into the usual numbness.

Not this time.

I wouldn't give in and simply tolerate ever again. I would fight for my survival every step of the way...go down fighting if need be.

It wasn't easy. There are a lot of things in this world that are probably tougher but I couldn't think of them offhand. I did it, though. I paid attention to every detail. Finally, it was over.

I returned home to pouring rain. I made sure the cats were okay, then threw on a rain suit to go check on the horses and pigs. A drain had clogged, flooding the horses' turnout. By the time I had it clear, I was soaked. I threw some fresh hay out for them and went inside for a bath. Barbara should be back any second.

I climbed in my tub and sighed with relief. There was a gentle tap at the door. "You in there, Lisa?" Good. Barbara was back.

"Make yourself at home," I hollered, "I'll be out in a couple of minutes and then it's all yours."

"Sounds great. I'll make some coffee." I heard footsteps receding.

I wiggled my toes and watched the water swirl around them. It was going to be nice having company around the house again. I wasn't accustomed to living alone. "It's amazing how much Barbara and I have in common," I thought. Smiled to myself. "Then again, maybe not." I liked the idea of having ancestors for a change. I'd have to ask her more about them.

That set me thinking. Since Barbara knew the names of people in her time, maybe we could hire someone who did genealogical research to find the others for us. I wondered if it were possible...if we gave them first names and an era. I raised up and pulled the plug. Sounded pretty far-fetched, even to me.

I still ran it past Barbara when I went in the kitchen. She had brought what appeared to be every candle in the house into the kitchen and lit them. I poured myself a cup of coffee and took a sip. Nice liquid sand. "Like candles?"

Barbara smiled, a little embarrassed. "All my life rainy days made me sad. Sometimes, in Louisiana, the rain can set in for weeks. Once, it rained for thirty-nine days and thirty-nine nights. The preachers were raking in the money and predicting the end of the world. I was never so glad to see the sun as when it peeked out on the fortieth day. I would always ask the servants to bring me extra candles and I would fill my room with them. It helped keep the gray away."

"Looks pretty." We smiled at each other. "I'm glad you're moving in."

Barbara winked a ladylike wink. "I am, too." She straightened and said, "I've got to work out the logistics of the move. I think the only thing I need, really, is my clothing. Nothing in that house means anything to me."

"Can you have your housekeeper pack them up and ship them to you?"

"That's a thought. However, do you know if it's A.M. or P.M.? I lose track."

We both thought. "I think it's P.M. The sky is dark and it should be light by now, even with the rain. I lose track, too. Maybe it'll be easier when the days get longer."

"Perhaps." Barbara mused. "Yes, it is because you can look for the sun." Barbara rinsed her mug and put it in the drain rack. "I'm going to bathe and then I'll call my housekeeper."

I poured out my coffee and rinsed my cup. "I'll get us a fire going. We can toast our toes and discuss contacting the others." I looked around the kitchen. "Mind if I blow out a few candles?"

Barbara grinned, looking at me from under her eyebrows. "Will you help me carry some to the greenhouse?"

"Woman, you are a trial."

"Now you're speaking my language!"

Arms akimbo, I wagged my head at Barbara. "Just how many is *some*?"

Airily, Barbara tossed over her shoulder as she headed to the greenhouse, "Seven."

"Ah." I grabbed two candles and followed. "Whatever works."

Barbara passed me, going for another load. "Whatever works."

We got her all set up and candles placed so they wouldn't singe any plants or burn the place down. Barbara said it was raining too hard for the house to burn anyway. I swear, sometimes *I* felt like the Granny.

When I went to blow the rest of the candles out, I hesitated. I blew out all but seven and took those in the living room with me. Seven points of light in the darkness. Seven women surrounded by that darkness. I shook myself and thought, "Quit giving yourself the heebie-jeebies and build a fire."

Having something to do took my mind off feeling sorry for myself. I settled in Fleming's chair to watch the flames. I let my mind drift.

Out of the blue, I heard Fleming say, *"... 'nother time line."* I froze. Looked carefully around the room. Nope. No visual Fleming. I stood up and looked behind me. Nothing. I turned and looked back at the fire.

Barbara walked in noiselessly and said, "Anything wrong?" startling me so badly I yelled and jumped a foot. That scared Barbara, so she screamed. Cats went flying in all different directions at once. It's amazing how four cats can seem like a hundred when they're all scared. Pandemonium ruled momentarily. When the dust settled, Barbara and I looked at each other with a shaky laugh.

"Aren't we a tad nervous?" Barbara sat in my chair, now her favorite. I mentally dubbed it her chair from this moment forward.

I sat in my and Fleming's chair. As far as I was concerned, it would always be mine and Fleming's. "You won't believe what just happened." I told her about Fleming's appearance this time and while I was at it, the last time as well.

Barbara was fascinated. "Do you mean he has actually managed to contact you twice? I was taught that was impossible."

"I was, too. This time it was like he was on a cell phone that was cutting out. I only got the end of what he said."

Barbara got up and paced in front of the fire. "It must be incredibly hard for him. I wonder if he meant to say *another time line*?"

The light filled my mind like the rising sun. "Barbara! He means for us to walk in another time line! How many can you walk now?"

She stopped and looked at me. "Two."

"Same here. What if we taught ourselves to walk in one more and kept it a secret?"

Barbara began to glow. "And used it to find the others?"

"How, though?"

"I'm not sure yet. I need to think. I've got the beginnings of an idea." She sat back down. "You know how we follow images of thought back to the place we left?"

I leaned forward. "Yeah."

"What if we could follow theirs?"

"Ooh, girlfriend. I think you're on to something. Follow them from where, though?"

"That's what I've still got to work out. There must be a way."

We sat silent. The fire crackled and the rain drummed on the roof. "It's not going to come to us right away." Barbara stood up. "I'm going to call my housekeeper. Phone in the kitchen all right?"

"Sure." I got up and threw a log on the fire. I started to sit back down and decided against it. I thought about housework I could do while Barbara was on the phone.

Barbara walked back in.

"That was quick," I said.

"The phone's been disconnected."

I sat down after all. Barbara hovered. "My house is more than likely closed. I had money in the bank for operating expenses. The accounts are probably closed, too. I'm destitute, Lisa."

"Do you think SoulJumper did this?"

Barbara covered her eyes. "He's the only one who could have. He deposited money every month to the account and had signing privileges. What am I going to do?"

I got up and put my arms around her. "The first thing you're going to do, Grandma," this brought a snort "is stop worrying." I led Barbara to her chair. "Fleming did manage to buy a life insurance policy when we married. I'm not rich but I can afford to take care of us."

"Forever is a long, long time, Lisa."

"We'll invest. As time goes by we'll find other ways of making money. Someday, I'll have to sell this place and it's worth a small fortune."

"Lisa…"

"Besides, you don't eat much, do you?"

Barbara smiled wanly. "I can get by with what clothes I have for now."

"Good. That's settled. Because we have more important things to worry about."

"Such as, how SoulJumper intends to destroy us?"

I nodded. "I think we can safely say that's next on his agenda or he wouldn't have closed your house."

Barbara dropped her head in her hands momentarily. Looked bleakly at me. "I have no idea how they would do it, do you?"

"No."

"What concerns me is, why?"

"Why what?"

"Why they are suddenly so willing to destroy us. If it was so hard to find us that they had to cheat, why are they so willing to let us go?"

Oh. Looking at it from that standpoint, I began to get worried too. "What you're thinking is, they've found a way to replace us."

"That's it in a nutshell."

I had a vision of a daughter I'd never seen, with Fleming's eyes.

"We have to stop them."

* * *

We sat for a while, neither of us coming up with a plan or even a decent idea. The fire burned low and I didn't get up to stoke it. Barbara stirred. "I'm not getting anywhere. I think I'll go lie down and try to sleep. It might clear my head."

I tried to remember the last time I'd slept. I'd gotten to where I didn't think about it anymore. I missed the escape. "You know, Barbara, that sounds like a plan."

We both slept until just before our control times. Luckily, there wasn't much for me to do in the middle of the night. I made sure the fire was out and the doors locked.

I went to a regular client in ancient Japan and to present day Australia. As I submitted to being washed and dressed, I kept trying to come up with ideas. We didn't have much time, I was sure. I was led to two bedrooms, totally different. In Japan, the client was waiting. He wasn't too horrible; he simply enjoyed older women. Although not for their conversation.

In Australia, I was alone. I tried to expand into another time line. Reaching out mentally, I searched. I pushed and prodded the edges of the time line that contained me. I felt my consciousness thin out.

The door opened and I jerked myself back. Frustrated and exultant all at once, I brought my attention back to the moment. I almost had it! As my body gave itself to the john, the part that was me began to plan. Next time I would do it. I had to know where I wanted to go.

Time is not like a river, it's more like the sea. All around us in every direction, flowing, constantly changing and never changing. Once you start jumping time lines, you can end up anywhere if you don't know what you're doing. I didn't want to ditz around, I wanted to go to one spot. That's why focusing my attention during control times turned out to be such a good idea. It disciplined me and prepared me for being in a new time line alone.

Under my own power.

When I returned home, I took a calendar down and divided the remaining days of the month in half. It took me a minute to figure out what day it was but when I did, I wrote A.M. on the top half. If I filled in the proper half on each return, it wouldn't be so hard to keep up. At least until the days got longer.

I couldn't lose myself in misery anymore. I had a daughter to protect. That's why Fleming was trying so hard to contact me. I was sure that was who SoulJumper and Sharon were after. A reality existed in which we had that daughter, Fleming and I. Probably the one I was taken out of the night I was chosen. Which meant that I most likely could not go back. My realities were full. I now existed outside my own life.

But I would deal with that later.

I glanced at the clock. Six-thirty and no Barbara. What was up with that? I got up and went through the house calling and looking. Nope. Nowhere.

I didn't like this. I didn't like this at *all*.

Finally, a little after seven, she showed up. I was as frantic as a zhombie gets. I had decided to take out my worries in housework and was scrubbing the toilet. I heard a tiny little "hi," looked up and there she was. I was so relieved, I jumped up and hugged her. She hugged me back. "They lengthened my control time."

"I know. Go sit, let me rinse my hands, I'll be right there."

I looked for Barbara in the living room but she was sitting in the kitchen. The rain had stopped and sunlight was streaming in the windows. Barbara looked forlorn.

"Would you like some coffee? Chocolate? A bath?"

Barbara shook her head and her hair flashed red and gold in the morning light. "No thank you. I may take a bath in a minute." She stared out the window. "If they increase our control times, that gives us less time to contact the others. Eventually, they may be able to control us twenty-four hours a day. Then we'll never be able to contact anyone."

I sat down. "Why do you think they only increased yours?"

"I think we're dealing with amateurs."

She never ceased to amaze me. "Amateurs."

"Yes. Well, maybe not amateurs exactly but they've only got partial knowledge. Just like we only have partial knowledge, the same is true of them. They know a lot more than us but not everything." Her eyes clouded. "Plus, we were a rush job."

I wiped at a spot on the table with my hand. "That would make them a loose cannon."

Barbara looked at me, thoughts elsewhere. "I just keep coming back to the fact that if they could do something, they would. Like SoulJumper didn't stop us from being together. If he could have, he would have."

"So, they're desperate."

"They have to find a way. Even if it's one they're unsure of, they have to try."

Chapter Seventeen

I went to clean the horses' tank and while I was refilling it, I remembered I had news for Barbara. She was in the tub when I went in, so I made my bed. I got done and knocked on the greenhouse door.

"Yes?"

"Come on out. I need to talk to you."

"Be right out."

"I'll be in the kitchen."

Barbara came in a few minutes later, wearing her lounging pajamas and robe. I took one look at her and said, "Go get dressed."

She stopped, looking at me quizzically.

"We're going to buy you some clothes."

Barbara grinned from ear to ear. "My goodness, you sure do know how to cheer a girl up."

I waved a hand at her. "Yeah, yeah. We're taking my car this time."

We shopped and forgot about everything but being girls for a while. We tried on ridiculous outfits and gorgeous outfits. Sales people watched us warily. We dithered and giggled until noon and finally staggered out of the mall loaded with bags. As we snapped our seat belts in my truck, Barbara said, "Thank you, Lisa."

I patted her hand. "Anytime, Grandma."

Barbara pinched me on the thigh and I poked her. This was so much *better!* We sillied ourselves out and I began to maneuver the truck out of the parking lot. When we were on Highway 1 and up to speed, heading from Monterey south to Carmel Valley, I said, "I've got some good news for you. I worked on going into another time line."

Barbara bounced in her seat. "Tell."

"I was left alone for a few minutes and I almost had it. I came back when the john opened the door."

"Can you do it again?"

"Yep. As soon as I have an opportunity. And this time I won't get frightened back like a rabbit. I have to decide where I want to go." We stopped at the light at the mouth of the valley and I looked over at Barbara. "I've been giving this a lot of thought this morning and it may actually work in our favor if they lengthen our control times." The light changed and I followed traffic onto Carmel Valley Road. "For now, anyway."

Barbara looked out at the passing scenery. "Because we have more time to practice?"

"Barbara, I realized something today. A reality exists in which Fleming and I had that little girl. That's why he's trying to contact me."

Barbara turned away from her window, her eyes filled with sadness. "There's nothing to go back to?"

I met her eyes, then looked back at the road. "There's nothing for us to go back to. We are zhombies and always will be. The smartest thing for us to do is be the best zhombies we can be."

Barbara roused herself and smiled. "You sound like an advertisement for the military."

I hooted and said, "Right now, we can't walk in other worlds unless we are under control. Let them expand our control times while we learn. Then when we free ourselves, we will know how to use our powers, how to *be* zhombies." We pulled in the driveway, parked and I turned the truck off.

Barbara sat still for a second, then started collecting bags. "We've got to return the rental car tomorrow."

We walked toward the house. "You're avoiding the point. What's bothering you?"

As I let us in, Barbara sighed and said, "I just don't like giving up any more of me. What if they extend their control and we never get free?"

We dumped bags on Barbara's bed. "We're not going to let that happen."

Barbara stopped opening bags and searched my face for an ounce of fear.

"You're right, my dear Great-Great-Granddaughter, we are not."

* * *

In reality, I was terrified. Same as Barbara, the idea of being under sexual slavery 24/7 for all eternity scared me silly. I didn't want to give up any more of me, either. My very next control, my time was increased by an hour. The next, another hour. Barbara was up to three hours over, each control.

We talked about it and decided the wise thing would be to prepare. I called an old friend and hired her son to caretake my farm and house. I told them Barbara was a relative from the lost branch of my family and I was going back to Louisiana with her. Probably for a very long while. I set up my accounts so my friend and her son could sign on them and hired an accountant. At the rate our control times were increasing, we'd be completely gone in a week. I made arrangements for my friend's son to move in.

Barbara and I talked whenever we could. Our fear bonded us. We discussed ways to find the others, a point we hadn't resolved and compared notes on our progress in a third time line.

We were both able to open ourselves into a third time line now. It was a lot harder alone. We discovered how much power SoulJumper actually had, how he had facilitated travel for us. We could get ourselves into a third time line but not in the events of it. We watched as if through water and no one was aware of us. Which was a blessing, because we kept popping up everywhere. We never knew where we'd turn up.

Then I managed to get myself to present day Detroit. It didn't do me any good, I had no idea how to find Anna but I *got* myself there. Barbara was thrilled.

We hardly ever saw each other now. SoulJumper and Sharon were keeping us apart, probably until they had Barbara and I under complete control.

Soon, we were. I existed in a nebulous world. I was moved from place to place, into a myriad of times. No more could I escape. No more baths or cats or horses to distract me and remind me beauty still lived. I felt myself slipping away. The toughest thing I ever did was to stop it. I wanted so badly to let go, find some place to hide. The fact was, there still *was* a me. That had to be good. I was under full control and I still had a part that was *me*.

One day, I went into a third time line and discovered that I could exist there outside what was happening in the other two time lines. I don't know why I hadn't thought of it before. I guess I was too busy being miserable. For some time, I didn't even practice expanding into more lines; that's about my only excuse for not doing it sooner. I finally got fed up and went. The bliss of being alone! And left alone! After that, I practiced all the time.

At first, I would have to come back to the other two time lines whenever I changed location. Then I got strong enough to incorporate the third reality and take it with me. I was free in my third time line. Truly free. But what good is freedom when you don't know how to use it? I was sure I had power but what power? How did I make all this work? I felt so ignorant. I needed a zhombie instruction manual: *Zhombies for Dimwits*.

I finally saw Barbara again. We were in San Francisco, in the gold rush era, in a mansion on Russian Hill. She looked so beautiful! I'd forgotten how beautiful my great-great-grandmother was. We managed to make eye contact once, in a hallway. She was leaving a bedroom and I was going in the next one down. As I met those incredible eyes with my own, for just a split second, I felt a light wash over me. If I'd had sensation, I would have described it as warmth. I saw from the surprise in Barbara's eyes she felt it, too. Our bond was still intact.

I looked ahead again and *there was Sharon!*

Watching.

She looked different and I realized she had her hair done for the period. A little more bouffant, still bleached blonde. No cigarettes or gum at the moment, full breasts pushed up over the top of her dress, almost exposing the nipples. An everyday floozy, found everywhere in the gold rush days.

Except for the eyes. The eyes were pools of nothing. No stars in that night sky.

And they were watching me.

I walked toward Sharon, seated in a window seat at the end of the hallway and felt as if I walked toward my doom. I had to keep my mind blank; if I let a single thought leak, she would pounce on it. I didn't dare let her find out I was in a third time line. I prayed she hadn't noticed what had passed between Barbara and I but I was afraid she had. I felt I'd never reach the end of that hallway.

I eventually did and turned into an exquisite bedroom, john following. Even with him between us, I felt those eyes boring into my back. The part of me that was in a third time line watching was laying low. I was afraid to come back, afraid I'd catch her attention. I felt a wind start to blow. I looked up at the sky; I think I was in ancient Egypt; and I saw Sharon's eyes staring at me. The wind blew harder. Sand swirled around me and still those eyes stared. Suddenly, I felt the wind pick me up and blow me like an empty candy wrapper. I tumbled and bounced. Worlds passed in a kaleidoscope on the edge of my vision.

When the wind quit blowing and I stopped, it was silent. *So* silent, not a sound. There was gray all around me. It was of me and I was it. I was nothingness and even lost contact with my other selves. I was alone and who knew where or when?

"Find your way back from there," Sharon hissed in my ear.

* * *

I berated myself for being stupid. I should have known Sharon and SoulJumper would be watching closely the first time they put Barbara and I together again. I'd really put the fat in the fire. What now? I tried to look around me and center myself but there was nothing to see. Only gray. I felt it swirl around and through me. It began to take me away, bits at a time, like oil drops on a stream. I became less of myself and more of the grayness.

I was frantic.

I reached out for the rest of me that still existed in the two time lines, one in San Francisco and one in Portland, Oregon. Nothing. I felt more of myself slip away into the grayness. I didn't have much consciousness left. I thought of Barbara. "I'm sorry, Barbara!" I cried into the nothingness that whisked me away. The gray entered my mind and began to dismantle my thoughts. "Fleming! Love you…"

I heard Fleming say, "I love you, Lisa." I tried to rally my being that was swirling slowly, relentlessly away.

"Think of Barbara."

I used every bit of self-discipline I had to focus on that voice. It sounded so much like Fleming! It was like pulling in a net of fish…mentally I pulled on all the pieces of me that were floating away.

"Lisa, think of Barbara. Take yourself to her." Fleming's voice came from everywhere. My mind felt as if I was on the verge of sleep. I gathered up the edges and tried to picture Barbara's face. Oh, this was so hard! The grayness muffled me and made me want to let go. No more struggle, no more anguish…nothing. The promise of respite lured me. I tried to

97

focus on an event. Barbara and I shopping together; arms linked, going to get her bedroom set up.

The grayness abated. I felt a little strength return.

I pictured Barbara as I had last seen her – no, no, that wasn't right. That brought sadness and the mist slipped back in. Not Barbara the zhombie. Barbara the essence. The actual Barbara. I struggled to bring her image to mind. It had to be so clear that I felt I could reach out and touch her. The grayness kept seeping in. I used every speck of energy I had left to make Barbara so real that I would be with her.

The instant I did it, I was with her.

She was in her third time line, sitting by a stream. She looked at me in surprise. "How on earth did you get here?"

"It's a long story." I glanced around. "Where are we?"

Barbara patted the ground beside her. "I'm not really sure. Won't you join me?"

I glared at her, all impatient, on fire to do *something* and then thought, "What?" I sat. "Sharon saw us make eye contact."

Barbara raised her eyebrows. "Sharon? Where was Sharon?"

"That's right. You had your back to her. After I passed you, she showed up at the end of the hall."

"Uh-oh."

"Uh-oh is right. She found me in my third time line and sent me someplace very unpleasant. Fleming helped me get back."

"Fleming? How?"

"He told me to think of you. I had to work out the particulars but when I did, I came here."

"Sharon knows you can walk in a third time line. It seems to me she would deduce that I can, too. I guess she hasn't come after me because she thinks she took care of you."

"I still have to connect with my other two time lines. I've been cut adrift."

Barbara tossed a pebble in the stream. "I wonder how she did that?" She turned to me. "What if you stayed that way for a while?"

I shook my head emphatically. "No. I'm afraid it might be like our original time lines. If I don't get all of it back together as soon as possible, I might not be able to. I'm a part of those two lines."

Barbara still gazed thoughtfully at me. "True. We understand so little. We can't be sure what might happen."

"The thing that disgusts me is, I have to picture them vividly to go there."

Barbara gave me a rueful smile. "Ignorance can, indeed, be bliss."

"Well Little Darlin'," I drawled as I stood up, "It's a case of mind over matter."

"Is that so?" Barbara stood beside me.

"Yeah. If you don't mind, it don't matter."

"Cute." Barbara looked pensive. "Um."

"Um what?"

"Will you be able to do this again? Find me in my third time line?"

"More than likely. It might take a couple of tries."

"Good." Barbara straightened her shoulders and shook back her hair. "It would help if we can meet in a third time line. We can work on finding the others."

I gawked at her. "You are *so* smart! I was going to rush back without even thinking about whether I could do this again. You're thinking this visualization technique may help us find the others."

Barbara batted her eyelashes at me. "Flattery will get you everywhere. Let's go get you put back together. But watch out for Sharon."

"*You* watch out for Sharon! You're the one who never saw her!"

Chapter Eighteen

I got reunited with my other parts with no problem. The thought energy was still strong and it brought me right back into the fold. I didn't know if I was correct about the energy dissipating but I wasn't prepared to find out. I didn't see Sharon or Barbara. Sharon probably left. No reason to stick around if the part of me that was being naughty was out in the middle of never. Barbara was probably in a room.

In the Portland reality, a door opened and Anna was led in. She was seated and waited docilely, eyes never leaving the carpet. I located a book on the table in front of me. I could pick that up if she raised her eyes. Maybe she would see me. I sat, willing Anna to look up. When she did, I almost forgot what I was doing.

She had Barbara's eyes.

The most astounding little beauty, she had ebony skin and green eyes.

I reminded myself I had a job to do and reached for the book. I lifted the book and set it back down. Anna looked at me with our great-great-grandmother's eyes. A woman came and took Anna by the hand, leading her to another room.

She had met my eyes. Only for an instant but she had done it.

I was snatched rudely to two time lines in the future. I didn't see Anna or Barbara in either one. Drat. There was still the third time line. If Sharon thought the "me" that was there was out of commission, I was safe. Right?

I thought of Anna. The one who had looked into my eyes. I separated myself into a third time line, pictured Anna and found her in a meadow. A black and white pony grazed in the distance. Anna was reading *The Secret Garden*.

"Hi," I said.

Anna started, dropped her book and stared. Oh boy, another pair of *those* eyes. I thought one set was enough.

Anna sized me up. "Hi."

"Can I sit with you?"

Stare. Silence. "Yeah."

I sat facing the same direction as Anna but not too close. "That your pony?"

"Umhum." Still not trusting.

"I have two horses. Rosie and Traveler. Rosie because she's red and Traveler because he covers a lot of ground real fast."

"That's Billy."

"Nice name." We sat and looked at the pony for a while, content to do just that.

Anna shifted so she could look at me. "Why did you come here?"

I looked back. "I came so I could talk to you."

Anna savored that. "Why?"

I looked at Billy. "This sounds stupid but to ask you if you want to be free."

Anna laughed. "You're right. It does sound stupid." Suddenly she didn't seem eight years old.

"Anna, how long have you been a zhombie?"

Anna sobered. Sighed. "Eleven years."

"How do you deal with the fact that you don't age? In your original world, I mean."

"I don't live there any more. My Mama thinks I'm dead."

My heart ached for Anna and her mother. "Do you live any place in that world?"

Anna shook her head. "No. Not for a while. That's why I started coming here."

I understood all too well. I was forty-nine, though. She was only eight. My anger hardened against the ones who had done this. "Anna, you know you can't ever go back, right?"

She nodded, green eyes fastened on my own.

101

"You can be free, though."

"What would I do?"

Kids always went to the heart of the matter. I thought. "You could come live with Barbara and me."

"Who's Barbara?"

That's right. Anna wouldn't know Barbara's name. I described her.

"Oh."

We looked at Billy some more.

"How do I know you wouldn't sell me, too?"

I had to quit underestimating this young woman. Physical age had very little to do with anything anymore. "You don't. I can tell you what Barbara and I have worked out; fill you in on everything we know or think. Then you can make an informed decision."

"Okay."

Definitely a woman of few words. Unlike me. I told her everything, ending up with, "Barbara and I believe it will take all of us to free ourselves. We don't know how it's done but we thought we'd get over the hurdle of finding everyone first. Then go from there."

"I know how to find Rachel."

I gaped at her. "You do?"

"I used to see her a lot. Not so much any more. We would talk when we could."

"You can speak when under control?"

"Umhum. Rachel can, too. Not as much as me, though."

"Did you teach yourself all of this?"

"Yeah. I got bored." Our eyes met. Anna went on, "So the first thing I did was teach myself to go someplace else. Then I met Rachel. When we realized we were alike, both zhombies, we started trying to communicate. Then she started meeting me here."

I shook my head in amazement. "You both can walk in a third time line. I'm assuming you only had two before."

"Yeah."

"Does anyone else know that you can?"

"No. I was afraid they'd stop me."

I snorted. "They wouldn't stop you! They'd book the extra time!"

"Yeah. I was afraid of that, too."

I didn't know what to say. I found it very sad that this girl was wise way beyond her years. I didn't say anything for a minute. "Do you want to try an experiment?"

"Maybe."

"We could try to go to Barbara."

Anna shook her head. "I'm not going anywhere with you."

This wasn't going to be easy. "Then why don't we try to call Barbara to us?"

Again, Anna shook her head. "Rachel. If you want to call somebody, we'll call Rachel."

"I don't know Rachel. I can't visualize her."

"I can. Promise you won't hurt her?"

And Rachel was there. Dark hair straight to her shoulders, petite. Sleek, like a cat. Hazel eyes, thank goodness. I didn't have to deal with another set of the Sheridan eyes. Rachel looked from Anna to me in surprise. "Who's she, Anna?"

"Lisa."

Rachel stared, interest dawning. "You're Lisa. I've heard about you."

I stuck out a hand saying, "Pleased to meetcha," and stood there feeling like a fool. Surely I could have said something more eloquent!

Rachel smiled and took my hand. "My pleasure," she murmured, teasing me with her eyes. Daring me to laugh. I did. Rachel laughed, too, a sound like bells. Anna watched, then joined in. Billy lifted his head and looked at us. Went back to grazing.

We sat in a circle in the lush grass. Anna picked a blade, put it between her thumbs, clasped her hands over it and blew air through it, causing an eerie whistle. "Where'd you learn to do that?" I asked.

"One of my uncles taught me."

Rachel met my eyes and shook her head ever so slightly. Subject taboo. Had this kid *ever* had a decent life? Rachel spoke up. "What are we all doing here?"

Before I had a chance to speak, Anna said, "Lisa says we can be free."

"Oh?" Rachel looked at me. "Is that true?"

"We think so."

"Who's we?"

"She and Barbara," Anna supplied.

"Anna," Rachel said, "I think we'd better let Lisa tell us all about it."

Anna stood up. "She's already told me. I'm going to ride Billy." She ran across the field, slowing to a walk when she approached the pony. He raised his head and whickered softly at her. Anna stroked his face and hopped on; no bridle, no saddle.

"She okay like that?"

Rachel nodded. "She's been riding him like that all along."

I laughed. "I know trainers that would love to hire her."

"Yes," said Rachel soberly, watching girl and pony, "But will she ever get the chance?"

I turned back to Rachel. "Let me fill you in and you can tell me what you think."

* * *

"So the angelic one is our great-great-grandmother," Rachel said. "How did you figure all this out?"

I stretched my legs out. "Barbara got most of it out of SoulJumper before we met. He had a soft spot for her and used to visit her."

Rachel chortled. "SoulJumper! How perfect."

I chortled back, "Yeah but I don't know if it helps anymore. I'm sure Sharon has told him about the nickname by now. I think they can sense us talking about them even if we don't use their names."

Rachel mused. "Probably so. We send out the energy and they pick it up. Like some sort of strange TV set."

"We have to be careful."

"Yes," Rachel said, "Gray is not my color."

I giggled. "I can't wait for you to meet Barbara. You two are a lot alike."

"Stands to reason."

"Yeah, well, if anyone can explain to me why y'all got all the looks, I'll be a happy camper. I got left out in that department."

Rachel looked me over appraisingly. "I wouldn't say that. You're quite pretty."

If I could have blushed, I would have. I changed the subject instead. "Do you know any of the others?"

Rachel leaned on her elbows. "Who's left? We've got you, me, Anna and Barbara."

"I'm not sure. I think Louise and Natalie."

"That's only six."

I thought. "Cynthia! Louise, Natalie and Cynthia."

"Have you ever met them?"

"No but Barbara has."

Rachel stood up, brushing off her bottom. "I think it's time we called Barbara."

I pointed with my chin at Anna and Billy, galloping at the edge of the meadow. "What about Anna? She didn't want me calling anyone she didn't know."

Rachel smiled, eyes on Anna. "She'll be okay with it now I'm here."

"Can you visualize Barbara, Rachel?"

"I think so. At least her hair."

"That'll do." We grinned at each other.

"How dare she?" Rachel asked.

"She says it's natural, too," I said, smirking.

"Oh, that's even worse!"

We straightened up and concentrated. Soon Barbara stood with us. "Oh, it's *y'all!*" Barbara came and gave me a hug. "I felt this urge to go and I followed this wonderful energy that came and got me. I wasn't sure what I'd find." She turned from me and went on, "You're Rachel. Is anyone else here?"

"Anna," Rachel answered, motioning with a hand toward the other end of the meadow. Anna had noticed Barbara's arrival and was riding toward us.

"How did y'all manage this?"

I explained how I had found Anna and Anna had called Rachel. By this time, Anna rode up, slid off the pony and said, "Hi," to Barbara. Barbara smiled and said "Hi," back.

Anna stared. "You have my eyes."

Barbara laughed. "No, sweetie, you have mine."

Anna laughed back. Barbara looked around. "Is this your place, Anna? It's pretty. Do you know where we are?"

"Seventeenth century France."

Barbara and I gawked. Rachel smiled. "Tell them where you got the book, Anna."

Anna crowed, "I stole it from a john!"

Anna cavorted in a little dance around us. Rachel still smiled serenely. As for Barbara and I, we were dumbfounded. I finally found my voice and stammered, "Can you both go to specific places and move things from one time line to another?"

Rachel shook her head. "No. Anna's way ahead of me."

Barbara and I stared at Anna, still doing her little dance. Barbara asked, "Anna, how did you learn to go to specific places?"

Anna shrugged. "I dunno. I got bored."

Barbara nodded. "And you just went. Do you think you can show us how?"

Anna stopped cavorting. Thought. "Sure. It's easy."

Ah, for the outlook of a child.

Rachel spoke up. "That's what *she* says. She's been trying to teach me the last couple of times I've seen her here. Without much success."

Anna started laughing. "Once, she ended up in a gladiator pit! With lions! She took *me* with her, too. I had to get us out of there quick!"

Rachel laughed. "Can you imagine what would have happened if those lions started tearing into us and we didn't bleed? Or die?" We all snickered. I considered telling about the time the prince in ancient Japan discovered I didn't bleed and decided against it. These were tales of freedom. I'd wait till I had one of those.

"Well, ladies," I said, rubbing my palms together, "I propose we all sit down and compare notes."

"That's a good idea," Barbara said, "Tally up what we know."

"First things first," I said when we all had a comfy spot, "Don't get caught in your third time line."

Rachel said, "The virtue is, we know how to get back now." Anna and Barbara nodded in agreement.

"Easy for you to say," I said dryly, "But true. Be prepared, though, Sharon may try something else."

Barbara spoke. "What book were y'all talking about, Anna?"

"*The Secret Garden.*" She got up, found the book in the grass and brought it to Barbara.

"One of my favorites," Barbara told her. She opened the cover. "First edition, too. Worth a pretty penny. How did you get it out?"

Anna sat close to Barbara. "I just pretended it was part of me."

That was putting it simply.

Rachel said, "This all seems to be more effortless than we understand."

Barbara nodded vigorously. "Because we tell ourselves it can't be done."

"Exactly." Rachel leaned forward. "We are still living in our old worlds in our minds. Rationale tells us how to picture our reality."

"Rationale and training," Barbara put in.

"The trouble is, we don't know what reality is out there," I said. "We are living in a world we know nothing about."

Barbara said, "Ignorant as a child."

We all looked at Anna. What separated her from us was fear...her lack of it. Anna shrugged at us. "It's easy. The time lines are different colors."

From out of the mouths of babes.

Chapter Nineteen

I sat up straight. "Something's happening. In one of my other time lines."

"What?" Rachel asked. All eyes were on me.

"There's a man. He says he knows what I am. It's in the future somewhere. I have to go back." I looked around at the only family I had anymore. "I'll find you again."

I heard Barbara say, "Be careful, Lisa."

I was in a living room, white on white. I sat in an armchair in a corner. A small blonde man with a mustache sat in an armchair facing me.

"I'm Ric," he said.

I sat, unwilling to move. He hadn't done anything to trigger a response and I didn't want to give anything away.

"Can you answer?"

Still I sat, staring at the floor, waiting.

"I know about Two-Feathers and Sharon."

What was this guy, some sort of futuristic vice squad? Now I *really* was going to clam up!

He sighed and ran a hand through short, spiky hair. "I don't know what to say to you."

That was honest.

"No matter what I think of to say, it sounds idiotic."

I'd certainly been there before.

Voices approached us. Ric glanced up, frustrated. He stood and took my hand. "Come with me." He led me to a bedroom that was all midnight blue with a hologram of the night sky on the ceiling. He flipped a switch and it seemed as if the sun rose in the room. Nifty.

Ric turned me around and seated me on the bed. I began to unbutton my blouse. He reached out a hand and stopped me. "That's not why I brought you back here."

Surprised, I lifted my eyes to his.

"Ha! I knew you could do it!"

I dropped my eyes again. This guy knew way too much.

Ric craned forward, leaning to put his face in front of mine. Meeting my eyes. "I know what you are because they made me, too."

That got my attention. I raised my head and met Ric's eyes.

"I'm not from this time. I'm from yours. I was the first zhombie Sharon and Two-Feathers made."

He must have sensed my disbelief because he said, "There are men who prefer men, you know. And women who pay for sexual servicing."

Okay.

Ric sighed. "Then they discovered the *Maternal Circle of Power*. Luckily, it took their attention off me. I kept my mouth shut and learned. We all used to live together, so I had plenty of opportunity. I just played dumb and they both said more than they should have in my presence."

"And?"

Ric smiled. "You can speak! Good. I wasn't sure."

"A little. Working on it."

Ric patted me paternally. "It took me years. Like I said, Sharon and Two-Feathers were so caught up, they didn't notice me. I was gathering information and storing it. One day, I overheard them talking about Sharon freeing herself. Two-Feathers asked, "Aren't you worried he'll catch up to you someday?" Sharon laughed and said, "No. He'll never get out of where I put him." I hid in the shadows, waiting for them to say more but they didn't. I did find out two things: There is someone with a reason to hate Sharon; someone knowledgeable; and she put him someplace to free herself."

I gathered all my energy and said, somewhat indistinctly, "Sent me someplace once."

Ric studied me. "You got back, evidently. How?"

"Fleming. Said think Barbara."

"Fleming? Who's Fleming? I know who Barbara is."

"Late husband."

Ric understood immediately. "They killed him somehow. You can't have any ties, anyone who loves you, for their *Circle* to work. Ties to a human life can be strong enough to take you back if you know what you're doing."

It hurt when I heard that. Too late for me. "You...free?"

Ric shook his head. "No. There are two more of me, out there working."

"Three...time lines?"

Ric looked at me, not understanding for a moment. "Oh! You mean can I walk in three time lines? Four."

"Impressed."

Ric laughed. "How many can you walk?"

"Three."

"Two for them, one for you?"

"Yes."

"Would you come someplace with me?"

Distrust raised its head. "Where?"

"I have a place, a house on St. Simon's Island, Georgia, in our general time. I'd like you to come there with me so we can talk."

I grinned. "...have to lead."

Ric said, "Have to lead...oh! You mean I'll have to lead! You haven't learned the time lines are different colors yet?"

Disgruntled, I shot Ric a dirty look. "Just did." Thank you, Anna!

"Does that mean you'll come with me?"

"Yes."

Ric took my hand and I separated myself into another time line. We were outside looking in. The next I knew, we were standing before a picture window, looking out at a stormy

Atlantic Ocean. I looked around me. Wood walls and floors, coral drapes, off-white couch, loveseat and two chairs. A bouquet of white roses with tiny coral sweetheart roses stood on a coffee table. I could see a well-appointed kitchen that opened onto a dining room with a huge antique oak table and chairs. A hallway with thick emerald carpet led to bedrooms on the other side of the house. "This is beautiful, Ric."

"Thank you." He smiled, motioning me to a chair. "Won't you sit? Would you like anything? Coffee? Tea? Do you eat?"

I sat down, shaking my head. "No, thank you. Sometimes I eat and drink but not often since I've been under full control. No reason to."

Ric sat on the couch. "I have a regular life here, so I keep food around. I support myself, quite well, I might say, as an antique dealer. It explains my disappearances and pays the bills."

"I should think so, when you can bring things back from the past."

Ric leaned back, crossing his legs and spreading his arms across the back of the couch. "There are certain advantages to being what we are."

"That's an interesting way of looking at it," I said.

"Hey, there comes a time when you say to yourself, I'm dealing with what's on my plate."

"True." I didn't want to say I'd preached the same sermon at Barbara.

"I simply made the best of a bad situation."

I looked out at the ocean; whitecaps and lightning. "Have you met any of the others?"

"All of them but they don't all know about me."

"That's an understatement. What's next?"

"I'll help all of you if you'll help me."

"What do you want?"

Ric gave me a Look. "Same as you. Freedom."

"That's all?"

"That's all! Isn't that enough?"

"I mean, no other strings attached?"

Ric studied me. "You've been dealing with Two-Feathers for too long."

"Yes, indeed, I have. Any time with him is too long. I call him SoulJumper." Ric snorted. I looked Ric over and made a decision. "Okay, I'll trust you."

"Good. Because I want to introduce you to your daughter."

* * *

The ocean roared and lightning flashed, unintentional punctuation to Ric's words. I laughed, bitterly. "I have no daughter."

Ric smoothed his eyebrow with his pinkie. "Yes, my dear, you do."

I didn't like this at all. I had a feeling I knew what was coming and I did *not* want to hear it. "You got any coffee?"

Ric looked at me in surprise. "Coffee?"

"Yes. I need a prop."

Ric laughed and hopped up lightly from the couch. "Of course. Come with me to the kitchen?"

"No." I met his eyes. "I need a minute."

"Sure."

Ric went in the kitchen and I got up and paced, watching the lightning flash over the Atlantic. So I did have a daughter. And, *agony*, I'd be willing to bet Ric had met her. Not only had they gotten my great-great-grandmother and me, they had gotten my daughter.

Oh, Fleming, I'm so sorry!

I don't know how much time had passed when Ric returned carrying an exquisite porcelain coffee service on a tray. He had included a matching plate of finger cookies. I procrastinated by not looking at him as I took a cup of coffee and a dish of cookies. We sat on the couch and Ric put his arm around me. I shrank away.

Ric said, "Oh, don't worry about me, I'm not into women."

I turned, searching his eyes.

"No, it's not easy for me when I have to be with women. I'm not even bi. But how much of this is easy?"

"You're preaching to the choir, Ric."

He squeezed my shoulders. "I know, honey. I should have been more sensitive."

Lightning flashed and thunder rumbled. The storm must be coming our way. I didn't remember hearing thunder before. "It's okay, Ric." I took a deep breath and reminded myself to breathe. "I'm ready to hear about my daughter."

"Are you sure? We don't have to talk about it now."

"They took her, didn't they?"

"Who? The demonic duo?" Ric asked. "Yes."

I grimaced. "Is she one of the *Circle?*"

Ric nodded.

I sat trying not to crumble in a million pieces. It was one thing to suspect, another entirely to know. Breathe, Lisa. "Which one?"

"Cynthia." Ric took his arm from my shoulders, picked up my hand and began massaging my palm. "It's Cynthia. They took her right before Barbara."

This was too much. I groaned. "She's been a zhombie for over ten years?"

"Yes."

"How many time lines can she walk?"

"Four." Ric looked uncomfortable.

I saved him the trouble. "Three for them and one for her?"

Ric's eyes scooted away, then back. Clear, clear blue, like an icy mountain lake. Not the eyes to be the bearers of bad tidings. "No, sweetie. They own all four."

I felt as if I was floating outside my body hearing this. "Is there anything of her left?"

"Oh, yes. She's in there but like us all, afraid to let it show. They've had her under complete control for so long, it's like looking at a woman encased in crystal."

"You say woman, Ric. How old was she when she was taken?"

Ric looked sad. "She was fifteen, hon."

I dropped my head and stared at the floor. "You know one thing I hate about being a zhombie?"

"What?"

"I can't cry."

"You got that right! I haven't had a good cry in years!" Ric patted my hand and stood. Lightning flashed, momentarily spotlighting rows of waves marching to shore. Thunder rumbled so I didn't hear what Ric said next. I raised my eyebrows and pointed to my ear. "Eh?"

Ric smiled and said, "I'm going to change. Are you all right? Need anything?"

"No thanks." I gestured to my coffee and cookies next to the roses. "I haven't touched what I've got."

"I have women's clothes, if you'd like to change. I think my things will fit you."

I smiled. "Thanks, Ric, you're sweet but I'm fine."

"Suit yourself." Ric went off down the hall to the bedrooms.

I sat with my head in my hands and tried not to think about who Cynthia looked like, Fleming or me. Barbara had said she had brown eyes...she got those from her Dad. Mine were hazel. Cynthia...that was the name of Fleming's last surviving aunt who died and left us the money to purchase the insurance policy. Also the name of one of my best friends in school. I'd always liked that name.

Oh, Fleming, Fleming. How did our lives unravel so completely?

Ric came back, saving me from myself. He was wearing dark pink velvet lounging pants and a softer pink silk oversized blouse with sequins and pink seed pearls sewn in the yoke. I nodded approvingly. "You look pretty."

Ric slithered in a perfect imitation of a runway model and said, "I've got the cutest little heels with pink velvet roses on the toes that go with this outfit but I didn't want to shock you." He waggled a bare foot at me.

"Shock *me*, Ric?"

Ric changed the subject, probably to keep me from becoming maudlin. "You don't remember the time I dressed you, do you? In San Francisco?"

I stared. "That was you?"

Ric smirked. "Yes. Looked good, didn't I?"

"Yes you did. What I remember thinking was that you had better taste than the madam who was dressing me in New Orleans that same control."

Ric laughed delightedly. "Yes *ma'am!* I am living dead proof that queens have the best taste!"

I laughed too. Whoo! That felt better. "Thanks, Ric."

He winked at me, sat in a chair and crossed his legs. "That's what friends are for," he said comfortably.

"You know," I said, "That's the time I met Barbara."

"Yes, I know. I saw you two, standing like statues, staring at each other."

I gasped. "You saw? Did anyone else?"

"No." Ric poured himself a fresh cup of coffee and checked mine, which I still hadn't so much as touched. He "tched" took the cup to the kitchen, dumped it and poured me a fresh cup. "Drink. It'll fortify you. No one else saw you because no one else realized you weren't supposed to be making eye contact."

I obediently took a sip of coffee. "It doesn't matter. We got caught, anyway. That's why they put us under complete control."

"Oh, no." Ric took a delicate bite of cookie. He and Barbara would make a great pair, they ate just alike. Ric was shaking his head. "No, they would have done that anyway.

116

They did all of us that way, starting with partial control and working up to total."

"Barbara says they're amateurs."

Ric snickered. "That's putting it succinctly. Having seen them in action, I'd say they are relatively new at this. I really think a lot of what they've done has been dumb luck."

I took a bite of cookie. It helped me to chew; stopped me from clenching my teeth. "You know, it's kind of a sorry state of affairs, to have sexual slavery in multiple worlds inflicted on us by a couple of doofuses who have fumbled their way to the top of the dung heap."

Ric hoo-hawed. "I never thought of it that way but thank you for calling it to my attention! That makes me feel so much *better*." He tee-heed and said, "Actually, they do both have quite a bit of power. I don't want to mislead you."

"But they are searching for knowledge, too?"

"They're searching for knowledge, too."

"Ric?"

"Hmmm?"

"What does my daughter look like?"

"She's a lot like you. Would you like to meet her?"

Boom!

A huge crash of thunder almost scared me out of my skin. I was so enrapt, I had forgotten the storm. I gathered up my frayed nerves and set my coffee down in case it happened again. By some miracle I had managed not to spill it. I looked over at Ric who was mopping coffee out of his lap with a napkin.

"Now I'll have to change clothes! Soon as I'm done, I'll take you to Cynthia."

Boom!

Another huge crash of thunder. "Do you think Mother Nature is trying to tell us something?" I yelled to Ric's back as he sashayed down the hall.

"Probably! But we aren't listening!"

Chapter Twenty

Ric came back in gray wool pleated pants and a lavender oxford cloth shirt. This time he had shoes on; black – and probably Italian – loafers.

"I'm definitely going to let you pick my wardrobe from now on, Ric."

He looked at me curiously. "Do you have one?" I laughed and Ric said, "Wait! Wait! That didn't come out right! What I meant to say is, do you have a home base?"

I explained about my little farm in California. "I haven't been back since I've been under complete control because" I peered at him from the corners of my eyes "I haven't perfected specific locations yet."

"Oh but Lisa, your farm should be an easy one."

"Well, maybe so but I haven't made it back yet."

Ric grabbed my hand. "It's because you're telling yourself you can't," he said airily. "Are we ready?"

The next thing I knew, we were standing in an elaborate garden. It must have been at least an acre. Through the trees, I could see what appeared to be a castle. "Ric, where are we? In the past?"

"No. The future. This was a family castle for centuries until a rock star bought it. Cynthia lives here full time in one time line. For a while, anyway. She'll be moved before anyone notices she hasn't aged. She's relatively happy here because the rock star is usually gone. Sometimes Cynthia travels with her but not often. I brought us here at a time she's normally in the garden."

I looked at him appraisingly. "Dang, you're good."

He smiled smugly and walked down a path. "I know. I hear that all the time."

I snorted and followed. The path led us to an enchanting hillside; green, lush grass starred with poppies, daisies and bachelor's buttons. At the bottom of the hill was a grove of immense old pecan trees. Num. I wondered if my daughter had inherited my taste for pecans. Then remembered it didn't matter.

Ric was making his way surely through knee-deep grass and flowers. He came to a stop at mid-hillside and looked down. What was he...? Oh! I got up beside him and realized someone was lying in the grass, completely hidden. A nicely made young woman with lines like a Thoroughbred filly popped open huge velvet brown eyes.

Fleming's eyes.

Pink lips exactly like mine opened in a full-fledged grin, exposing teeth like mine.

"Ric!" She jumped up and gave him a hug, then turned to me. "Who'd you br..." Her voice faded away. I smiled weakly. "Mom?" she whispered. "Mom? What are you doing here?"

Then my daughter hugged me.

* * *

I vowed that first time I held my daughter I would not rest until I had set her free. We pulled back and looked at each other. My daughter! She had my hair, too. Naturally curly, fine and brown. She kept hers cut short in a cute mop. Fleming's eyes searched my face. "Mom, you look older."

I laughed joyously. "Nice thing to say to your mother!" Your mother! Your *mother!* I never thought I'd say those words in reference to myself. Cynthia laughed, too, a laugh all her own, impish and elfin. Ric stood back and grinned from ear to ear, watching us. "Honey," I said, still unable to wipe the smile off my face, "Let's sit down and we'll tell you everything."

A shadow crossed my darling's face. "We'll have to hurry because Anrica is due home."

"Anrica? Ah. Then you go under control?"

Cynthia wagged her head at me. "Mom, how do you know about control?"

All this time, Ric stood there looking innocent. I turned on him. "You didn't tell her anything?"

Ric shrugged, hands in pockets. "I thought she had enough on her mind."

Great.

I looked at Cynthia, trusting brown eyes fastened on me. Boy. How did I explain? Hmmm. "I'm your Mom but I'm not your Mom."

"You're from an alternate reality?"

Never underestimate your children.

"Yes, I'm from an alternate reality. One in which I never got to have you."

"Oh." Those eyes never flinched. She was a brave little thing, our daughter. "Did you know about me?"

"Not always. Ric just told me you were in the *Circle* a little while ago."

Her eyes dropped at that. "Are you? In the *Circle*?"

I nodded. "Yes, sweetheart, I am."

Her eyes met mine again, all shame gone. "I'd be embarrassed to talk to you if you weren't."

I said sadly, "I know."

Cynthia took my hand and sat cross-legged on the ground, pulling me down beside her. She patted the ground between us, saying, "Sit, Ric."

Ric sat, complaining about getting his pants dirty. Cynthia and I wrinkled our noses at him, saw each other and laughed. It was almost like watching myself in a mirror. Ric laughed at us laughing at each other. He was enjoying this almost as much as I was. We heard a gong in the distance.

I looked at Cynthia. "A gong?"

She grimaced. "Anrica's here."

Ric interpolated, "Anrica has delusions of grandeur."

Now I was really laughing. Cynthia stood up in one graceful movement. I lumbered to my feet and Ric hopped up.

"I've got to go," Cynthia said.

I gave her a hug. "I love you, honey. I'll see you soon."

She turned away, then turned back and looked at Ric. "Why did you go find my Mom?"

Ric returned her look steadily. "Because it will take all of us working together to set ourselves free."

Cynthia glanced from one of us to the other. "You guys think there's a way to do that?"

Ric and I said together, "Yes."

My lovely daughter gave Ric a hug. "Good." She turned to the house and again, turned back. She was looking at me this time. "Will we be able to go home?"

I looked askance at Ric. Maybe he knew something I didn't. He didn't meet my eyes. Bad sign. "No, Cynthia, we won't."

She thought for a second. "Can I come live with you?"

I smiled broadly. "Of course. Me and your great-great-great-grandmother."

True teenager, she struggled not to show anything but her eyes were shining. The gong sounded again.

"Cool," she said and was gone.

* * *

I watched my leggy daughter run up the hill. Such effortless grace! Ric cleared his throat gently. "We need to be going before someone sees us. Anrica doesn't like for Cynthia to have company."

"Poor kid," I said, reaching for Ric's hand.

He took us back to St. Simon's. The storm was over but the surf was still huge, roaring in like a multitude of buffalo. "You got a good sea wall, Ric?"

"Honey, this place is built on stilts." Ric was gathering coffee cups and cookie plates.

"Stilts?" I asked.

"Pilings sunk deep in the ground. It can withstand gale force winds." He went into the kitchen talking over his shoulder. "It'll make you seasick, though, because it sways."

"It won't make me seasick."

"Smarty. It makes my human friends seasick."

"You got friends?"

Ric came out of the kitchen and stuck his tongue out at me. I laughed. "I got no use for that."

Ric laughed, too and said, "It's got no use for you, either. Seriously, Lisa, don't you have any human friends?"

I sat on the couch. "Not anymore. All I have is you, Barbara, Cynthia, Anna and Rachel. I hope to add Natalie and Louise to my list soon."

He sat in a chair. "We'll have to teach you to have a human life. For now, we'll call Barbara."

"*Really?*" I squealed. "I know how to do that!"

"Poor baby. So ignorant. Shut up and think about Barbara."

I did. I thought and visualized until I thought I'd get a cramp. I looked at Ric. He sat with his eyes closed, a relaxed expression on his face. He didn't seem to be having any problems. I tried again.

No Barbara.

"Ric?"

"Yeah?"

"Don't you think she ought to be here by now?"

"Yeah."

I stood up. "What do you think?"

Ric stood, too. "I think I'd better go try and find her. Do you mind staying here alone for a few?"

"Not at all." I sat back down. "Hurry back, though."

"I will."

Durned if his grin wasn't the last thing to go!

*   *   *

Ric was back before I had time to get nervous. I didn't like what I saw in his face, though. "Bad news?"

"Afraid so. They've taken over her third time line."

"Oh no."

Ric paced in front of me. "We have to teach you to expand into another time line."

"Why? Sharon thinks I'm in cold storage."

"To keep you safe. This way, you've got an extra."

I sighed and shifted on the couch. "Is Barbara okay?"

Ric stopped and stared out at the ocean. The moon was peeking through the clouds, a tiny crescent. "She's as okay as can be expected. Once I've got you a fourth time line, we'll teach her." Ric started pacing again. Five steps each way, back and forth.

"Ric, stop. You're making me dizzy."

He perched on the arm of a chair. "I thought you didn't get dizzy."

"That's seasick. Is expanding into the fourth time line pretty much the same as the first three?"

"Yes and no. It's less forgiving."

"Well, I'm delighted. Less forgiving?"

Ric plopped from the arm of the chair into the seat, leaving his legs draped over the arm. "How do I explain this? When you go into your fourth time line, it's like graduating from elementary to high school. More is expected of you. You have to be on your toes, very aware and alert. If you aren't, it can carry you away to who knows where."

"I've been there," I said dryly.

"Yes and look what happened to you."

I snorted. "What?"

Ric smirked and said, "It gave you gray hair."

That got me. I started to giggle. Every time I tried to stop, I'd start up again. Ric waited patiently.

"Feel better?"

I took a deep breath. *"Yes."*

"Good," Ric said. "Let's get started."

I got up, raising my arms as if we were ballroom dancing. "I'm ready, partner." Ric grabbed my hands and we waltzed a few steps. Enchanted, I said, "You can dance!"

Ric dropped my hands and looked away. "Ric Stevens, ballroom dancer. I would have gone to the top."

Comprehension dawned. "You lost someone, too?"

"Yes." Ric's eyes met mine. "I'll take you to see him one day. I don't disturb him because his life has gone on. I just look at him."

I gave Ric a hug. "Come on, you. Let's get to work so we can get us all free."

Ric pasted a smile on his face. "The ABC's of a fourth time line are: always be careful," he chanted in a nasal tone.

"You sound like my first grade teacher."

He poked me in the ribs. "Pay attention or you'll have to stay after school."

"Yes *sir*!"

"And don't you forget it!"

Chapter Twenty-One

Ric was right. The fourth time line is less forgiving. Instead of getting easier with each time line from now on, it got harder. He had to grab me and pull me back several times so I wouldn't get swept away. While we were at it, he taught me to differentiate the time lines by color. It's not something done with the eyes but with the spirit. Your very being senses the vibratory differences and the brain interprets it as color. I was already getting better at specifics, even though I couldn't sense the time lines as well as Ric thought I should.

I took Ric to Anna's place in seventeenth century France on one of my first tries. I reasoned I was familiar with it and that would make it easier. It did, too. I took us right there.

No Anna, no Billy. Just a ruined first edition copy of *The Secret Garden* in the grass.

"This doesn't look good," I said.

Ric was walking around. "She was here last time?"

"Oh yes. So was her pony. I got the impression she stayed here all the time in her third time line."

Ric picked up the book and riffled through the swollen pages. "Sharon and Two-Feathers probably checked up on everyone when they found out about you. The only reason they haven't come after me is I'm yesterday's news."

I scuffed my toe in the grass. "They don't know we've met, either."

"We can't expect that state of affairs to continue. That would be a dangerous assumption. Once they've got everyone else in line, they'll be scrutinizing us."

"What do we do?"

"We set up blinds."

"Blinds? Venetian blinds?"

"No. Blinds of light, for want of a better term. They shine so brightly that we are camouflaged."

"Oh, that makes *lots* of sense."

Ric grabbed my hand. "You'll see. For now, though, let's go back to my house."

When we left our fourth time line and went back to our third, something dark went whizzing past us.

SoulJumper was waiting for us on the couch.

* * *

"Isn't this the happy couple?" he asked sarcastically. "Where have you two been?"

Ric smiled. "Tripping the light fantastic."

"Funny." SoulJumper shifted his dead gaze to me. "You don't want to learn, do you?"

"Actually, I do."

SoulJumper didn't move.

Ric said, "What do you want, Winston?"

Finally those eyes left me. "That's a stupid question."

Ric never flinched. "What would it take for you to not want it anymore?"

SoulJumper laughed, then leaned forward. "Are you trying to bribe me?"

Ric studied his nails. "If that's what it takes."

"There's not enough money in the world."

I spoke up. "So the *Circle of Power* is that important?"

"You'll never find out." SoulJumper stood and grabbed my hand in one swift movement. "You're coming with me. I'm not letting you out of my sight this time."

I felt myself starting to go when Ric took my other hand shouting, "No!" I was being pulled in two! I put all my energy into staying with Ric. SoulJumper was so powerful! I felt my hand slipping from Ric's. *NO!* I pulled my essence away from SoulJumper and tightened my grip on Ric's hand. One last pull, when it seemed I would surely rip in half and SoulJumper was gone.

Ric and I tumbled to the floor, still holding hands. "We did it!" I looked at Ric through mussed hair. "We *did* it!" Ric laughed exultantly. We hugged and rolled around on the floor like puppies. At long last, our jubilation subsided and reality set in.

"We've got to get out of here," Ric said.

"Where?"

We stood, shaking out our clothes and finger combing our hair. "Someplace we can hide," Ric took one last swipe at his spiky hair.

"Ric, what about your beautiful home?"

He gave a rueful smile. "Nothing lasts forever. I'll come back when it's safe and make arrangements to sell it."

"Oh, Ric."

He gave his shirt a hitch and said, "I knew it had to happen someday. And a lady never wears out her welcome."

"You sound like Barbara."

"Sweetie, I wish I looked like Barbara!"

"Don't we all."

Ric took my hand. "When we see her, we'll tell her what a hag she is. Come on. I've got an idea."

He took us to Barbara. We were in a mansion in Beverly Hills. It appeared to be about 1940. We materialized next to an elaborate swimming pool. Thank goodness it was dark. I asked, "What are we doing here?"

Ric started walking inside. "Looking for Barbara."

I stopped dead. "What?"

He tugged my hand. "Come on. They'll never look for us here." He paused to grin at me. "At least, I don't think they will."

I agreed to walk again. "I sure hope you're right."

"I am. Can Barbara speak under control?"

"Yes," I replied, "A lot better than me."

"That wouldn't be hard."

I jerked Ric's hand. "You never let up, do you?"

"Try not to," he answered. "Wouldn't want you to get lazy."

We walked onto a portico with soaring columns and statues of Greek gods and goddesses. "Impressive," I breathed. "Who owns this mausoleum?"

"You don't want to know. You probably like his movies. There's Barbara." Ric pointed with his chin.

She was seated on a plum colored divan, dressed in white and gold, hair cascading unbound down her back. She had a circlet of gold around her forehead with a single marquis cut diamond set in the center, like a third eye. She looked inward, unseeing.

Ric said, "Stay here." He looked around, walked over to the divan and kneeled. I saw him say something to Barbara. Her eyes snapped to me. Joy flooded those beautiful lifeless pools. Ric said something else and taking her hand, led her toward me. When they got to me, Ric said, "Keep moving. Pretend to be a client."

I fell in behind them. We went down the longest hallway I've ever seen and into an over decorated bedroom. "This guy's taste is all in his mouth," I thought and closed the door behind us. Then I hugged Barbara. She was weak, I could tell and tired of holding out against ennui. She shakily hugged me back. "Are you okay, Barbara?" I asked, searching her face.

"I'm very glad to see you. Who's this?" She gestured to Ric.

I gave her the details. Barbara listened quietly; none of us knew how much time we had. When I had finished talking, she asked Ric, "When can you teach me the fourth time line?"

We were sitting on the bed, Barbara in the middle. The door opened and we all looked up. A small, bald man with round glasses turned beet red and stammered, "I'm so sorry!" as he fumbled his way back out the door. Barbara giggled.

Ric glared. "Don't you two get going! We don't have time for frivolity!"

Barbara and I worked our mouths around and managed to look at him with straight faces.

"Better."

Barbara snorted. I choked back a guffaw. Ric crossed his arms on his chest. "I can see this is going to be a challenge."

"No, no, Ric, we'll be good, we promise!" we chorused.

"You'd better." Ric got serious. "Barbara do you have any idea how much time you have left here?"

Barbara shook her head ruefully. "None."

"Okay. I think I can get you back if we go into a fourth time line now. Trust me?"

Without hesitation, Barbara said, "Yes."

That's my girl!

Ric stood and held his hand out to Barbara, talking fast, telling her about the fourth time line. Green eyes fastened on blue, she drank up every word. Ric pulled me to my feet. "You get on the other side. Hold on so we don't lose her. Ready? Here we go!"

Before I could say, "Where?" we were there. I gaped at Ric. "Big Sur, Ric? Sharon lives in Big Sur!"

"I know," he grinned. "What kind of car does she drive?"

"Ric! You can't be thinking of…"

"Don't get your panties in a wad, sweetie, I'm kidding."

Barbara hooted. I frowned at them and said, "You two need to grow up."

We were standing on Garrapata Beach on an ultramarine blue day. The surf was clear green and white as it unfurled on the sand. I had to give Ric credit! "Ric, I want your technique."

"That's what they all say."

"Get your mind out of the gutter."

Barbara shook her hair in the fresh breeze and called, "Girls! Girls!"

Ric pointed at Barbara. "Now she knows how to treat a lady!"

129

I made a face. "Okay, ma'am, you got us here. What do we do now?"

"I thought we'd go to my house."

"Your house?"

Ric smiled smugly. "My house."

Barbara said, "Sounds wonderful to me!"

"Everybody grab hold!"

We went to a house overlooking the ocean just south of Garrapata. It stood high on a cliff. We were in the living room and walls of glass gave us an unobstructed view. Redwood beams supported the ceiling high above us and a loft tucked itself into the tallest point. Overstuffed chairs and love seats were gathered in front of a huge stone fireplace. Barbara gazed around enchanted. "I've never seen a house like this!" She stopped, mesmerized by the sight of the endless blue Pacific Ocean. "Oh, my gosh," she breathed.

I draped an arm around her shoulders. "Welcome to Big Sur, Granny. I never got the chance to bring you here."

"Oh my *gosh*."

I grinned at Ric. "She's got Big Sur-it is."

Ric smiled. I remember the first time I saw this area. I felt the same way."

Barbara turned to us, eyes glowing. "Lisa! Let's live in Big Sur!"

"All right," I replied dryly, "We'll just move in with Ric."

Ric snorted. "Too many women. Not enough testosterone."

Barbara put her hands on her hips. "Child, don't cross a southern woman."

He threw up his hands. "I give!"

Barbara laughed. "You betcha."

"Okay, so maybe you ought to think about making your base here for this time line," Ric said nonchalantly. "There's plenty of room."

Barbara pirouetted across the floor and latched onto Ric in a bear hug. He took her hands and danced her around.

Whatever step he was doing, she knew it and followed effortlessly. I laughed at their antics and sang nonsense in time with them. At length, they collapsed into overstuffed chairs. The sun poured through the windows and lit up Barbara's hair like a torch. Light. Blinds.

I sat on a loveseat. "Ric, what about those blinds? Do we still need them?"

"Oh yes!" Ric sat up. "We do. We should take care of that right now."

Barbara raised her eyebrows. "Blinds?"

"You could call them shields. That's probably a better term. What we do is surround ourselves with light. When Sharon and Two-Feathers come looking for us, they can't differentiate our energy from the surrounding light." He spread his hands and smiled beatifically. "Make sense?"

As one, Barbara and I said, "No."

"Okay." Ric stood up and did his five-step pace.

"*Ric,*" I said.

He glanced at me. "I forgot. Sorry." To Barbara, "It makes her dizzy."

Barbara appraised me. "No kidding." Green lanterns beamed back at Ric. "Go ahead."

"You know how we are beings of light and time is light and so is energy?"

I said, "Yes." Barbara nodded.

"We hide in that light."

Something seemed to penetrate. "I almost got it. You're saying because our energy puts off light, they can find us by that light."

"Ye-es."

"But if we take light from the energy around us and hide in it, they can't see us?"

"I get it!" sang out Barbara.

Ric beamed at us. "The hard part is keeping it there. You can't forget it for an instant."

"How do we do that?" I asked.

"It becomes a habit. At first, though, you have to think about it. Let's start at the beginning. The first thing to do is separate out as if we're going into another time line. Once you're outside this one, you'll be able to sense the energy. Try to see it. Pull it to you and cloak yourself in it. Then we'll come back here. *Remember to bring the energy back with you.* Make it part of you. Understand?"

Barbara and I nodded. "Do we hold hands, Ric?" I asked.

"Not this time. Barbara, can you do it alone?"

"I think so."

We stood in a circle, nodded at each other and went.

Chapter Twenty-Two

I stood outside the time line. I was alone. Ric was right, I could sense the energy. I emptied my mind, trying to see.

Oh, how beautiful!

I was surrounded by live, pulsating light. It was the color that reflects from a white dove's breast as it flies across a sunrise. For the first time, I got a visual on the lines, every color of the rainbow, vibrating and flowing. I could even *hear* the light. Music filled me; music I had heard in dreams. I reached out with my energy and drew light to me, wrapping myself in it. I waited until I felt like it had become part of me.

When I started to go back, I sensed the light diminishing. Once again, I waited. This time until every fiber of my being glowed with it. I made it back, shield intact.

Ric was waiting. "Dahling, you look mahvelous."

I flashed him a smile. "You too. Where's Barbara?"

"Not here yet." Ric blew on his fingertips. "I'll be right back."

He was as good as his word and had Barbara in tow. "Thanks, Ric. It's easy to get lost."

"I'm so good," he smirked.

"Yeah, well, don't wear it out," I said punching him in the arm.

"Hag."

"Sleaze." I headed for the woodpile announcing, "I'm going to build a fire."

"Then we all need to talk. We keep ending up on the defensive." Ric turned to Barbara. "While she gets her hands dirty, would you like the fifty-cent tour?"

She curtsied. "Why, sir, I'd be honored."

I turned back to my fire. Some people have all the luck. If I tried to curtsy like that, I'd fall over on my face.

* * *

By the time Ric and Barbara came back from their house tour, I had a roaring fire. We picked spots and sat. Ric asked, "Anybody need anything? Now that I'm sitting, I way as well get back up."

"Not I." Barbara tucked her legs under her.

"Nope."

"All right, then. You had your chance. Shields okay?" We nodded. "Great. Barbara, have you run into anyone else in your third time line?"

"Who? Oh! You mean Anna or Rachel?"

"Or Cynthia or Natalie or Louise?"

Barbara shook her head. "No. No one. I've been alone."

"What about the other two lines?" I asked.

"No one."

Ric said, "We've got to make contact with the others. I could go."

"I think I could find Anna," I offered.

Ric shook his head emphatically. "No, Lisa, we can't take the chance. I'd rather you two stayed here."

"Who will you try to find first? Anna's pretty accomplished," Barbara said.

"We know where to find Cynthia." Ric nodded at me. "Lisa can tell you about that. Make yourselves at home. I'll fetch Anna." He was gone.

I stoked the fire and cuddled back in my chair.

"You met Cynthia?" Barbara asked.

"Yeah. And do I have a lot to tell *you*. Remember that daughter I never got to have?"

"Cynthia?" Barbara was astounded. "That means they got three of us in a direct line."

134

"Uh-huh. I wonder what that means to their *Circle of Power*? Does it strengthen it or weaken it?"

"Maybe weaken it."

"How?"

Barbara mused. "Oh, I don't know. Like inbreeding."

"Incest is best."

"I'm going to wash your mouth out with soap," Barbara said absently. "On the other hand, what if it strengthens it? The more closely related, the stronger the *Circle*?"

Ric appeared with Anna. She gave a cry of joy at seeing us and we had a group hug. "Have you been to my spot? Have you seen Billy?"

I looked over at Ric. "He and I went but Billy was gone."

Anna sat on a loveseat, looking sad. "They took me away and wouldn't let me say goodbye, even."

Barbara moved to sit by Anna and smoothed the hair from her face. Anna looked up at her with anguished eyes, saying, "I don't know what happened to him."

"I know, honey," Barbara soothed, "We'll find him." She stared earnestly at Ric over Anna's head.

"If you can find him, we can put him on my farm in Carmel Valley. My caretaker won't mind one more."

Ric gaped at us in astonishment. "You have got to be joking. You think I can bring a *pony* back with me?"

Barbara nodded serenely. "Yes indeedy do."

Ric snorted. "That's what I call blind faith. With the emphasis on *blind*. You ladies are delusional."

"I bet we all could do it," Anna piped.

"Yes, Ric! Anna's right! It could be our first task!" I exclaimed.

Ric said sourly, "I'll make y'all a deal. Let's get all of you here and then we'll go get the pony." He lightened up and smiled. "All we have to do is leave Anna here so she doesn't run into herself and go to a time before they took her out. We'll explain to the other Anna what we're doing, snag Billy and we're outta there."

I had to admit, I was impressed. "I agree."

"Me too," from Anna.

"And I," Barbara said.

"Great. Now that's settled, who should I go get next?"

"Rachel!" shouted Anna gleefully.

Ric pinched her cheek playfully. "Anything for you, sweetheart." He twirled around, snapped his fingers and was gone again.

"I *like* him," Anna declared.

"We all do," Barbara smiled.

"He won't hurt me 'cause he doesn't want to be with girls," Anna stated softly. "I like him."

"I swear," I told myself, "If it takes me the rest of eternity, I'm gonna see that child gets a better life." Barbara's eyes met mine and I could tell she was thinking the same thing. We smiled grimly at each other.

Anna had discovered the view. She moved across the floor like a sleepwalker, entranced. It was getting later and the light had changed the ocean from ultramarine to cobalt and violet.

"Wait till you see the sunset, Anna, it's gorgeous," I called.

She nodded, barely unhearing. Her nose was almost pressed against the glass.

"I think she likes it," I said in an aside to Barbara.

She chuckled. "I think so. Now if we can just get her pony here…"

I met her eyes. "Do you think we can?"

Barbara stretched luxuriously. "I don't know," she yawned at me, "But we'll surely try."

"That we will." We sat silently, watching Anna enjoy. "Where do you think Ric is?"

Barbara looked worried. "He does seem to be taking a little longer."

A door slammed. "Why did you pull away from me, Rachel? I told you to stay with me! We wouldn't have ended up in the front *yard.* Now my shoes are *ruined!*" Ric sounded irritated.

We heard, "Murmurmurmurmurmur."

"You'll have to have more confidence in yourself if you want to do *anything,* Rachel."

They were getting closer, so we could hear Rachel's answer. "Not everyone has your confidence, Ric. You should be more tolerant."

"Tolerate you all the way to the ends of the universe," he grumbled.

Barbara called out, "What's up with you two?"

Ric came in first and his shoes were a sight. Caked with mud, they didn't look like they'd ever be the same. Barbara tried not to laugh. "Just where did you two come in?"

"In the middle of the stupid pond!" Ric was disgusted. "Five hundred dollar Italian loafers, *ruined.*"

Rachel came in the living room saying, "Not the middle. Only the edge."

"Close enough," Ric snorted.

"For drama queens," I said snidely.

Rachel sputtered and Barbara gave up trying not to laugh.

Ric pouted, "I need understanding, not ridicule."

Rachel noticed the windows and was drawn as if by a magnet. As she passed one of the loveseats, Anna jumped out from behind it. "Boo!"

Rachel shrieked, then grabbed Anna, roughing her up playfully. "You little stinker!" She gave Anna a big loud smooch on the cheek.

Anna squirmed. "Eew!" and giggling, smooched Rachel back.

"As much as I hate to miss this touching reunion, I'm going to change," Ric sniffed, flouncing down the hall. Rachel, Anna and I looked at each other and snickered.

"What did you do, Rachel?" Anna whispered.

"I pulled when I should have pushed," Rachel whispered back, "And now I'm going to have to buy him a new pair of shoes!"

We howled.

From the back of the house, Ric hollered, "I hear you!" He came back wearing jeans, hiking boots and a sweatshirt emblazoned, *Monterey Fisherman's Wharf.* "I'm not ruining any more of my good clothes."

"Ric."

"What, Barbara?"

"Do you have something I could borrow? I'd love to change," Barbara wheedled.

"Oh, me too, Ric!" Rachel cried.

Ric stared at them, deadpan. "What's in it for me?"

"We won't steal them," Barbara said.

"Oh! Well! That's good enough for me! Come with me. I'll show you where everything is and you can take your pick."

He came back in a couple of minutes, alone. "There goes my wardrobe."

Anna and I laughed. I said, "Barbara has clothes at my house. Do you have a car, Ric? We could go get some tomorrow."

He nodded. "Yes but I want everyone here before we take any little excursions. I'm going to get Natalie and Louise next. I have to leave Cynthia until last because none of us has a fifth time line."

"I never thought of that."

"I've tried it," Anna said helpfully. "It's not that hard, just different."

I glanced at Ric, who was staring in amazement at Anna. "We told you."

Ric swallowed. "I'll say. How did you do it, Anna?"

"Well, when you go there, you have to stay in time with it."

"What?" Ric asked.

"It has a beat, like music. You have to go with it. If you don't, it doesn't work."

"You have got to be kidding me."

Anna giggled. "*No*, Ric, honestly. The first time I tried, I didn't know. It hurt."

"Hurt?" I asked.

"Uh-*huh*." Anna bobbed her head emphatically. "I came right back."

"But you went again," Ric said flatly.

"Umhum. Because it's fun."

"Fun?" I felt like a straight man! "What do you mean, fun? I thought it hurt?"

"*No*." Anna was disgusted with elder stupidity. "Fun to go places."

Barbara and Rachel came back adorned in Ric's splendor; Barbara in harvest gold silk loungers and Rachel in forest green linen. Rachel heard Anna's last remark. She said, "Anna, mind your manners," and to us, "I told you she was a natural."

"It's a given," Barbara said. We all turned to her. "Our barriers." She shrugged. "Think about it. Even at eighteen, when I was taken, I already had a mental picture of the world. An idea. We all know that picture isn't valid but it's still there, telling me what I can and cannot do. We learn it from birth, almost by osmosis. Limiting us in this world we inhabit now. Anna's mental picture wasn't fully formed yet. She hadn't had time to be taught. So her mind is more open, accepting new concepts readily that our minds have trouble comprehending. We have to clean out our old thoughts."

"Including the majority of what our creators taught us," I said. "A lot of it was lies, to increase control."

"Exactly!" Barbara brushed hair out of her eyes impatiently. "It's like we talked about, Lisa, because we believe in it, our slavery exists."

"Yes but how do we un-believe?" Rachel asked.

"It's the ultimate brainwashing," Ric said.

"We have to build our own structure for our world," I said. "Talk about the blind leading the blind!"

Anna was getting fidgety. "I thought we were getting Louise and Natalie."

All eyes went to Anna. Poor kid looked like a deer in the headlights. She tucked herself behind a chair and peeked out at us. Ric said softly, "More like, the children will lead the way." He gestured at us to stop staring at Anna so she would come out of hiding. "Cutie, I will go right now and get Louise and Natalie. Then will you help me with the fifth time line?"

Anna sat in the chair and bounced. "Sure."

"Shake on it?"

Green eyes searched Ric's face. A little hand popped out. "Shake."

Ric turned to us with an elaborate bow. "Ladies, will you excuse me?"

"How long does it take him?" Rachel asked.

"Not long at all when he doesn't end up in the pond," I gibed. We laughed.

"Poor Ric," Rachel sighed, "He puts up with so much from us."

"Yes, I do," came from over by the windows. Ric stood there with his arm around an exquisitely beautiful blonde woman. A little taller than Ric, slender with natural platinum blonde hair falling straight to her waist. Soft bangs feathered above blue eyes with fawn eyebrows. She looked like an ice fairy. "I'd like you to meet my sister, Natalie," Ric said proudly.

"Your sister!"

"What?"

"You never told me you had a sister!"

All of us but Anna spoke at once. She stared, awestruck, at Natalie. "You're *beautiful*," she breathed.

Ric grinned like a possum. Natalie elbowed him in the ribs. "You'll never change," she said affectionately. "My brother loves his little surprises."

140

I glared at Ric. "We call him the drama queen." I smiled at Natalie and extended a hand. "Welcome. Do you know everybody?"

Natalie shook my hand with slender, elegant fingers. She might appear ethereal but she had a firm grip. "Mostly. By sight." She pointed as she called each name. "Rachel, Lisa, Barbara and Anna. We're only missing Louise and Cynthia."

Barbara asked, "Did Ric tell you what we're trying to do?"

"Yes. Gathering everyone to see if we can make the *Maternal Circle of Power* work for us. Ric," when she turned her head, her hair flowed like silk across her shoulders. "Are you going to get Louise and Cynthia?"

"Louise. We have to work on a fifth time line for Cynthia. All four lines she can walk are under control."

"Anyone done it?"

Anna emerged from her spell. "I have!"

Natalie smiled at Anna. "Good." I liked the fact that she didn't belittle Anna's intelligence. "Do I have time to go for a walk?" she asked Ric and then turned to us. "Please don't think I'm being unsociable, I never get to go outside. I miss it so much."

Ric laughed indulgently. "I really think she'd live under a tree if she could. She never used to want to come inside."

"Do you mind if I come with you, Natalie?" I asked.

"Not at all! I'd love the company. Let's go before we miss the sunset."

"Not too far!" Barbara called after us. "We don't want to have to come looking for you."

"Yes, Granny," I smirked. I dodged the pillow Barbara threw at my head and dashed out, Natalie following.

"Granny?" she asked when we were walking side by side. The sun was getting ready to set and a cool wind blew our hair. In the peach glow, Natalie's hair looked like liquid flame streaming behind her. The ocean and sky were Parrish blue and the sun set off a burst of lemon light that flashed up and down the horizon as it dropped, apparently, into the sea.

"Barbara's our great-great-grandmother," I said as we stood with the sunset glow on our faces. We turned to walk and the wind caught our hair, whipping it around our heads.

"Interesting."

"You know we're all related." We stopped at the cliff's edge to stare at the ocean, white foam against dark rocks in the gathering gloom. Someone had put a bench there, so we sat and drank in the beauty.

"Star light, star bright, first star I see tonight," chanted Natalie, pointing at a star brilliant in the deepening blue of the sky.

"I wish I may, I wish I might," I chanted back.

"Have the wish I wish tonight!" we intoned together and leaned into each other, laughing.

"What'd you wish?" asked Natalie.

I feigned shock. "I can't tell you, it won't come true!"

"You're as bad as my brother. He won't ever tell me, either."

"Must run in the family."

"Lisa! Natalie!" we heard Ric call from the house. "Get in here before the bogeyman gets you!"

Natalie sniggered. "*He's* the bogeyman! He was always scaring me when we were kids."

We got up and made our way up the path to the house. "Some things never change," I said.

Natalie went through the door. "Thank goodness."

Chapter Twenty-Three

Louise was as Barbara had described her and also warm and full of humor. She had dancing blue eyes and dancing feet, never seeming to be still. We made our introductions and settled all over the chairs, loveseats and floor in front of the fire. I had built a nice one; it was still roaring away but I threw on a couple more logs for good measure.

Barbara spoke first. "Before we start working on a fifth time line, is everything okay in everyone's other three?" She looked at Ric and I. "Primarily you two. Didn't you just run into SoulJumper?"

"SoulJumper? Who's that?" We had to stop and explain to Natalie and Louise but it was worth it for the kick they got out of it.

Ric spoke up. "We ran into him in our third time line. I'm thinking because we're not there at all right now, he won't be able to find us."

"Yes but won't he find that suspicious? That you're not in your third time line at all? Won't that lead him to deduce that you have a fourth?" Barbara asked.

"I've thought of that," Ric answered, "He'll probably think we're hiding."

"Don't assume he'll underestimate you, Ric," Natalie said, "He may not."

"Yes, Ric," I said, "We've already given him a couple of nasty surprises."

"All the more reason to take on the fifth time line," Ric said. "So why don't we get started? Everyone's other time lines are okay?" We all nodded. Ric turned to Anna. "All right, cutie, you're on. Show us how it's done."

"Ric, wait," I said. "Shouldn't Anna, Rachel, Natalie and Louise have shields?"

"I thought about that," he answered, "I think they'll be safe for now."

"No, Ric," Barbara put in, "We shouldn't take any chances."

"But will they be able to maintain them and learn the fifth time line so quickly?" Ric asked.

"Hold it, you guys," Rachel said, "What are you talking about? Why not tell us and let us decide?"

So that's what Ric did. When he had finished, the room was silent.

"I vote shield," said Rachel.

"Me too," piped Anna.

"Count me in," said Natalie.

"Uh-*huh*!" from Louise.

"Right, then," Ric said. "Everybody clear on what needs to be done? You'll have to go alone. I can only help bring you back if you get lost."

Four pairs of eyes fastened on Ric, four heads nodded in unison.

"Off you go."

Natalie was the first to return. "That was gorgeous!"

I agreed. "When I did mine was when I finally saw the colors of the time lines."

Anna came back next. "It was pretty!"

Ric grinned at her. "Did you bring it back with you?"

Anna hopped up and down in her excitement. "Uh-huh! And now I can hide where they can't find me!"

Louise returned. "I've never seen anything like that!" She shook her short brown curls reminding me of a terrier.

All right, where was Rachel? I looked at Ric. He sighed. "I know, I know. I'll go find her. Hopefully we don't end up in the ocean this time!"

Ric was only gone a moment. "I found her but she slipped away from me. Call her, everyone, I'll go back and look for her. "He disappeared.

We thought about Rachel and called her to us. At length, Ric appeared with Rachel in tow. Anna ran and threw her arms around Rachel's waist. "You scared me!" Anna cried.

Rachel smoothed Anna's hair. "I scared myself, honey."

"Did you bring your shield?"

"I think so." Rachel held out a hand and admired it. "Can't you see it?"

Anna giggled and released her stranglehold to stand back and look Rachel over. "No."

Rachel tickled Anna. "Then you're just not looking, are you?"

Anna giggled again. "I'm not ticklish!"

Rachel tickled some more. "No but your giggle box is!"

"Hello!" Ric hollered above the din. "Can we start on a fifth time line now?"

Barbara agreed. "Ric's right. Anna, can you take us all there?"

Green eyes locked on identical green eyes. "I think so."

"That's my sweetie." Barbara nodded reassuringly. "Tell us about it."

Then we locked hands and without really knowing why, stood in a circle. It was automatic. Seven of us here. Missing one component but a good number. We separated out and stood between time lines, then slipped into a vibrating pink/gold line. Immediately, I could feel a pulse.

SLAM! I was off the rhythm. SLAM!

Ow. I needed to do something quickly! Anna was right, this hurt and I didn't feel pain anymore.

SLAM! Another sledgehammer blow to my entire being. What was the secret here? SLAM! Breathing. Try breathing. I let the rhythm flow through me and adjusted myself to it. *Slam.* Well, that was better. I concentrated. Suddenly I was one with the rhythm and started to flow away! I thought of

Natalie and Barbara, who had been standing on either side of me and envisioned their hands clasping mine, holding me in place. I stopped floating away. I centered myself more and soon I could see everyone, still in a circle. We all breathed in rhythm. I felt a power start to build in the center of our circle, rising like a whirlwind between us. What was *this*?

I heard Ric say inside my mind, "I'll take us to Cynthia." I could tell everyone had heard him. The power in the center whirled faster, in rhythm with the indelible beat of the time line. I ebbed and flowed with it.

We were in the castle garden, on the hillside this time.

No Cynthia.

I looked at Ric. "She should be here any minute," he said in answer to my unspoken question. "We're a little early."

Sure enough, here came Cynthia, walking slowly, staring at the ground. Ric whistled. Cynthia raised her head, saw all of us and stood stock-still. Then she began to run in leaps and bounds toward us.

"I *knew* you would do it! I knew you would find a way! Mom! Ric!" She grabbed me and spun me in an exuberant hug. She let me go and latched on to Ric. "It's perfect! Anrica's gone for three weeks! Three whole glorious weeks!"

Ric grinned. "Would you like me to introduce everyone?"

"Oh! I'm sorry! I didn't mean to be rude. Please do."

Ric took care of introductions, then got brusque again. "Cynthia, do you think you could learn the fifth time line?"

Cynthia looked embarrassed. "I know it already." She wouldn't meet Ric's eyes.

"Why didn't you tell me?" he sputtered.

"I wanted it to be a secret. I wanted to surprise you."

"She got you, Ric!" Natalie hooted.

"I'm surprised, all right." Ric was miffed and proud at the same time. Proud won out. "You are *the* most amazing little witch!"

"You're not mad?"

Ric pretended to pout. "No. But you owe me, big time."

Cynthia laughed. "Put it on my bill."

"Shall we go to Big Sur?" Natalie asked.

"It's comfortable there and we can talk in relative safety," Rachel said.

"What's in Big Sur?" Cynthia asked.

"I have a house there," Ric answered. "Everyone agreeable?"

"Let's form a circle again so we don't lose anybody," Rachel said. Everyone turned to look at her. She grinned sheepishly. "Like me."

We muddled around, getting arranged and clasping hands. As soon as the last handclasp was made and our circle closed, I could feel the power. I glanced at the others. Oh, yeah. They felt it, too. Expressions ranged from awestruck to joyful amazement.

The power sang through me like liquid vitality. I vividly saw the whirlwind this time, like a miniature galaxy, stardust swirling and suns glowing from within, lighting it in subtle colors. It climbed upward to immense height, then compressed; climbed, compressed; never ending as waves on the shore. When we entered the fifth time line, *its* rhythm adjusted to *ours*. We flowed and ebbed and moved through the universe like solar wind. Life itself sang with our power. We walked with the stars and they guided our way. The time line embraced us. I realized I could see everyone more clearly than ever before. They were all glowing from within – a white gold light that dazzled but didn't blind.

Then it was over.

We stood in the living room of Ric's house in Big Sur and knew none of us would ever be the same.

We had experienced the *Maternal Circle of Power*.

Now we knew what it was all about.

* * *

There was no way SoulJumper and Sharon could allow us to live if we freed ourselves. They knew what we had better than we did ourselves. They would destroy us rather than allow us to possess it. And we would destroy them to keep them from getting it.

We all kind of tentatively fiddled around. I poked the fire, Barbara fluffed pillows. Ric went to make coffee with Natalie in tow. Rachel flopped on a loveseat and twiddled a lock of hair. Louise stood slack-limbed, resembling a puppet on loose strings. Anna sat next to Rachel holding her unoccupied hand and Cynthia wandered from window to window, gazing out at the darkness. We were exhilarated and afraid.

When Ric and Natalie came in bearing trays of coffee, juice and finger sandwiches, we descended on them like a flock of vultures. "For a bunch of zhombies, we sure are hungry," Louise cracked when we had taken a break from chewing.

"Dead men don't eat quiche," Ric said.

I almost blew coffee through my nose. Coughing and snorting, I choked out, "Ladies don't crack jokes when others have their mouths full!"

Ric managed, somehow, to be deadpan. "I never claimed to be a lady," he waited two beats, "Though I do lay claims to being something of a comedian."

"Ba-da-da-boom," I said, imitating a drummer.

"The hook! The hook! Bring out the hook!" Natalie cried. "Get this guy off stage before he empties the house!"

"Natalie, is Ric older or younger than you?" Rachel asked.

Natalie thumped Ric affectionately on the head. "We're twins."

"Twins!" Barbara cried. "Oh my gosh!"

"Yes, Barbara," I said wryly, "You can let the other shoe drop."

Barbara didn't bite. "*Y'all*! Look what we've got here! We've got great-great-grandmother, mother, daughter, twins and four more, all maternally related perhaps with unknown connections as well. See the structure? The pattern? I bet it takes all eight of us to make the *Circle*." She turned to Ric. "What made them choose you? You were the first, right?"

Ric nodded. "I always figured it was chance."

"I don't think so," Barbara shook her head. "I wonder how long they've been researching our family; how long it took to find us."

"Oh my gosh," Rachel gasped.

"Exactly." Barbara pulled her hair back, rolled it in a bun, then let it fall in a shower of light. "We met their specifications."

"They'll never let us go," Louise said.

I looked around at my family. Already they were so dear to me. I couldn't let SoulJumper and Sharon harm any of us any more. I knew I would fight to the death for our freedom and so would all they. It was the only thing we had left besides each other.

And the *Maternal Circle of Power*.

"Oh yes they will," I said grimly.

Green eyes, blue eyes, hazel eyes, brown eyes. All met. All genetically linked, all genetic freaks now. Accepting that to live even death-life, we might have to die. Whatever. We would face it together. Sharon and SoulJumper brought us here and made us, now they could deal with the consequences. Don't mess with a rattler unless you don't mind getting bit.

"Cynthia needs a shield," Louise said.

"Good idea," Ric said. "I'll get her going on it and y'all can clean up the dishes."

"Oh, *thanks*, Ric!" I said.

He wagged his head at me. "I cook, you clean."

"Hmmph! Gonna reverse that order!" Barbara grumped, gathering cups and saucers on a tray. We all pitched in and Cynthia and Ric wandered off where they could hear themselves think.

Louise sidled up to me when no one else was near. "Cynthia's your daughter?" she asked.

149

"Mm-hmm."

"She's cute."

My attention came to the moment. "You like girls?"

"Sure," Louise said nonchalantly. She tried her best not to blush. Losing battle! "Does shc?"

I do believe it was the first time Louise had ever been in love! I looked over at Cynthia, listening intently to Ric. "You know, sweetie, we just met, so I don't know her very well. Why don't you ask her?"

"She doesn't like that Anrica chick."

I smiled. "That doesn't mean she wouldn't like you. My advice would be to ask her."

Louise looked at me. "You don't mind?"

"Mind you asking her out?"

"Mind her being with girls."

I thought for a minute. I sensed Louise needed a serious answer. "I believe people of the same sex have every bit as much right to love as people of the opposite sex. It's just another path people walk. Not everyone is alike and I think it's unrealistic to think they should be. Make sense?"

Louise nodded. I handed her a full tray. "You can ask her when she gets done. For now, can you take these to the kitchen for me?"

I watched Louise walk away, thinking. Louise was a sweet girl. Cynthia could do worse. They were of an age and most importantly, they both were zhombies. I knew from experience how painful relationships between humans and zhombies could be. Oh well. Best thing for me to do was keep my nose out of it. Young love didn't require mothering.

"Cool!" I heard Anna squeal. "He's got a dishwasher!" I shook my head with a laughing sigh and walked in the kitchen. Just as the last dish was loaded.

"Perfect timing," I wisecracked.

"She just *loves* work, y'all," Barbara drawled, "She could sit and watch it for hours." She poked Anna. "Look alive, here comes a buzzard."

"Are you calling me a buzzard?" I challenged.

"No. Just lazy." Barbara dashed out of the kitchen before I could bonk her with something. Anna ducked past me, giggling. I wandered back out to the living room. "Where are Rachel and Natalie?"

"They went for a walk," Ric called from over by the windows.

"In the dark?"

"Oh, no. Come see."

I joined Ric and realized that because of the lay of the land and the house, he could see east. A full moon was rising over the Santa Lucias. A study in blue and white on velvet, it lit up the night. "Ooh," I breathed. "Beautiful."

"A witching moon," Ric teased.

I shot him a look. "Don't even think it."

Cynthia came back. "Now that's what I call a light show!"

Ric and I laughed. "Should I go get the others?" I asked.

Ric looked over the living room. Cynthia, Louise and Anna were chattering on the floor in front of the fire. Barbara was draped across a loveseat, lost in the flames. "I hate to interrupt such a peaceful scene."

"If we don't, it won't be peaceful for long."

"True," Ric sighed. "Go ahead. I'll stay here and lap up familial comfort while I can."

"I'm such a slave driver."

"Oo-oo! Can I borrow your whip?"

"It's not your color!" I headed out to get Natalie and Rachel. The night was enchanting. There was a soft breeze on my cheek and the moon was so bright I could see almost as well as in daylight. Far below, the ocean crashed against the rocks in an ageless beat. A coyote sang in the distance.

Rachel and Natalie were sitting on the bench at the cliff's edge, talking with dreamy expressions. The moonlight cast distinct shadows on their faces and I was struck by how similar their bone structure was. Such beautiful women – they must have known love before they were taken. How sad they'd probably never know it again. "Yoo-hoo!" I called from a distance so I wouldn't startle them, "It's me, Lisa." They scooted over and made room for me on the bench. "I'm supposed to be bringing y'all inside," I said as I settled myself comfortably on the hard bench.

"Yeah," Natalie sighed in contentment. "I guess we better go inside." She crossed her legs.

"What was that?" Rachel stared behind us.

"What?" Natalie and I craned our necks and looked too.

"I thought I heard something, like someone walking behind us."

"Okay, girls," I stood and turned toward the house. "Let's go. I don't like…"

"Lisa?" Natalie and Rachel stood and turned toward the house.

"Which was no longer there."

The finger of land where a solid structure of redwood and stone had stood only moments before was empty.

* * *

"Oh no," I groaned.

"Grab hands!" snapped Rachel. "Quickly! Grab hands so they can't separate us any more than we already are!" We grabbed hands. This was a new authoritative Rachel, you did what she said. "Don't let go for *anything*." I didn't think I could have opened my hands once I had a grip on theirs but we had no idea what we were up against.

Natalie asked, "Shouldn't we walk toward where the house is supposed to be?"

We looked at each other. Silence. Rachel nodded. "Let's go."

We walked slowly up the hill, holding on to each other for dear life. "SoulJumper and Sharon must have put us in an alternate reality," I whispered. "We need to visualize the house."

"What about the others, visualize them?" Rachel asked.

"Them too. You can bet those two know we're all together."

Out of nowhere, a shadow burst up at our feet with an inhuman wail and beat around our heads. I started to drop Rachel's hand to keep it away. "Don't let go!" She lifted both our hands and pushed at the shadow. "That's what they want!"

The blackness picked at my eyes with a thousand fingers and slapped my head from side to side. It wrapped around Natalie and Rachel and tried to enter their mouths. We fought desperately with clasped hands to keep it away. Natalie fell and Rachel and I yanked her to her feet almost before she hit the ground. Without thinking, I snatched Rachel's empty hand with mine, making a closed circle. The shadow screeched and flew up. It flapped over us like a headless Pterodactyl shrieking. The sound alone was enough to split your head. We held on tight. As suddenly as it attacked, it was gone. The night was quiet.

Too quiet.

No wind, no waves. Where *were* we?

We stood in a huddle, trembling, still in our little circle. "That seemed to help, Lisa, when you closed the *Circle*. Even with only three of us, it appears to have power," Rachel said.

Natalie giggled nervously. "Yeah but we can't walk like this."

"I don't think we need to be walking," I said. "Notice there's no sound of surf? The full moon's gone too. See how dark it is? There's no telling where we are."

We fell silent, peering into the darkness and listening for all we were worth.

No good.

"Any suggestions?" I asked.

"Stay in the *Circle* and visualize the others?" Rachel answered with a question.

"Does anybody else feel anything?" Natalie asked.

"Specify anything," I said.

153

"Is the ground moving?"

Now that she mentioned it, the ground did feel funny. Like it was liquefying.

"It's pulling me in!" Rachel screamed. Living quicksand, the ground was reaching up for our feet and now our legs and sucking us down. It boiled under us and extended itself even higher. We rocked back and forth trying to keep our balance. We tugged our feet out and as soon as we set them down again the morass began to devour them.

We struggled to hold hands – if we let go we were lost – and remain standing. There was no sound except our frantic cries. We seemed to be locked in a vacuum and the ground attacked us in total silence. I noticed something on my face and realized that whatever it was had made it to my face. It felt as if it was spreading roots and growing. I tried to brush it off with the hand joined with Natalie's but our arms were covered.

Rachel cried, "It's all over me!"

I drew our *Circle* tighter and we huddled, terrified, being tossed like toys on the roiling earth.

"Natalie!" I yelled, "Think of Ric!"

"RIC!" Natalie wailed. I didn't expect her to do *that*. "RIC HELP!"

I called Barbara.

"Anna!" Rachel joined in.

Still, our voices were the only sound. It was eerie – being swallowed in total darkness and silence. We held tighter and called louder.

I heard something.

"Shh! Listen!"

Way off, like seabirds crying in the wind, I could hear voices. Faint – ever so faint but *there*. I willed them closer; willed us closer to them.

"Natalie! Lisa! Rachel!"

It was! Ric and the others were calling us! "Hear that?" I asked excitedly.

"Yes!" Natalie and Rachel cried. We really started yelling then!

Oh no. We were falling! Slow motion, we drifted down like leaves. I felt my head hit the softened earth and it began to fill my eyes, nose and mouth. Faintly, I heard Cynthia say, "You're not taking my Mother from me again."

I was lying on blessedly rock hard ground, drenched in moonlight, gazing up at my daughter's lovely face. Barbara's appeared next to it. I never saw such a beautiful sight in my life!

"Can you sit up?" Barbara asked.

I sat up. "Yes." We were a few feet from the bench at the cliff's edge. I realized we were alone. "Where are the others?"

Barbara and Cynthia exchanged glances. "They haven't come back yet," Barbara said. "Ric's gone to find them. What happened?"

I shot a look toward the house. Yes! It was there! "They sent us into an alternate reality where the house didn't exist. Then somewhere else from there."

"They?" Barbara asked.

"The very ones." I nodded. "They know we're here and they know we're together."

"Not good," said Cynthia.

"Not good at all," I agreed.

Ric appeared. "I can't find them!" He was frantic. "Lisa, do you have any idea…?"

"None." I shook my head. "It was dark and silent and the ground was devouring us. That's all I know."

"Ground!" Ric snapped his fingers. "That's why I can't find them, they're buried!"

"Ric, the *Circle* had power with only three of us," I volunteered. "Why don't we try that?"

Ric turned to Cynthia. "Would you run in and get Louise and Anna?" Cynthia took off and he said to Barbara and I, "We may as well do it here. This is where y'all disappeared from, it might help to be at the exact spot."

155

Cynthia came back with Louise and Anna in tow. "What do we do, Ric?"

"We all join hands, close the *Circle* and call Natalie and Rachel." He smiled nervously. "I guess."

We formed the *Circle* on the cliff's edge with the ocean roaring below us and the moon watching over us. I pictured Natalie as I had seen her in the sunset and Rachel laughing with Anna. The minutes ticked by. Still we stood, giving it all we had. "There they are!" I shouted. "I feel them! Natalie, Rachel, we're here!"

Everyone started calling "Natalie, Rachel!" until it sounded like a chant. "NatalieRachelNatalieRachel" we intoned. They appeared, clutched in each other's arms on the ground for a second and were gone again. We concentrated a n d   c h a n t e d   h a r d e r , "NATALIERACHELNATALIERACHEL."

Finally, they were with us. We were afraid to break the *Circle*, so Barbara called out, "Can y'all stand up?" Shakily, Natalie and Rachel untangled themselves and stood. Our *Circle* collapsed in on itself, everyone hugging and talking at once.

Ric yelled above the melee, "Everybody in the house! And what ever you do, *stay together*. No more splitting up!"

We moved up the path in a chattering horde, some still holding hands, scared to get more than an arm's length from each other. I don't know why but we all, even Natalie, felt safer once we got inside. We huddled in the living room.

"Okay, folks," I announced, "From now on, one of us goes somewhere, we all go. I don't care if it's to the next room."

"A giant organism," Louise murmured.

"You got it. We are going to have to be one close family unit," I said.

Rachel said, "It seems to be our only protection."

Cynthia shifted in her seat. "So much for shields."

"Yeah, Ric, what about our shields?" Natalie asked.

Ric shook his head dejectedly. "I don't know what happened."

"Who taught you about shields?" I put in.

"I overheard."

"Mmm," I said, "Seems like anything from them is suspect."

"The Trojan horse theory?" Rachel asked.

"That and the fact that they are misusing the knowledge they have. We've learned a distorted form of it," I said.

"What do we do?" Natalie asked. "We don't have time for trial and error."

"We have something they don't," Cynthia said.

"The *Circle*?" Louise asked.

"Yes." Cynthia nodded eagerly. "That's got to mean something."

"How do y'all think they use it?" Rachel asked. We all looked at her. "We have to be together. We have to hold hands and we have to close the *Circle*. They don't do any of that. How do they utilize the power?"

"That, my dear Rachel," Ric stood and bowed to her, "Is a very intelligent observation." He picked up her hand and kissed it. "Very intelligent."

"Better than usual?" she grinned impishly at him.

"Infinitely," Ric grinned back. "How do you suppose they utilize it?"

"Through one of us," Anna said in her clear voice.

Ric spun to Anna like a game show host. "Ding! Correct answer!"

"Through one of our other selves?" Rachel asked.

"More than likely," Ric answered. "They must get a watered down version of the *Circle*. Still powerful enough to make them do anything to possess it."

"Including destroying our lives," I said, thinking of Fleming. I looked around the room. We all had our memories. My gaze stopped at Cynthia. Wide brown eyes met mine and I was grateful I had the chance to know her. Even under the circumstances. I blew her a kiss and she smiled and blew one back.

"Including destroying *us*," Ric said flatly.

Chapter Twenty-Four

"It's time we did something," I said belligerently. Everyone nodded and a chorus of "Yes!" went around the room. "I'm tired of being at their mercy!" I declared, "It's their turn to suffer!"

"You said it, sister," Ric said. "Got any suggestions?"

"We're the ones with all the power supposedly," I said, frustrated, "Why don't we use it?"

"How, Lisa?" Rachel asked.

"I don't know! Why don't we just try something? How about we call SoulJumper here to the center of the *Circle* and see how he likes that. Put him on the hot seat!"

"And then do what with him?" Ric asked. "We can't just turn him loose."

"They're always sending me somewhere, I'd like to do the sending for a change."

"That's basically a good idea, Lisa," Ric said approvingly, "But it has two flaws. One: You've always gotten out. Two: We have no idea where to send him. They know what's out there and we don't."

"I'd like to find someplace awful," I grumbled.

"Make one up," said Anna.

"Oo-oo," crooned Louise.

"That's *good*," said Natalie.

"My darlin' Anna, you have done it again," Ric said in a terrible brogue. Natalie punched him and he grinned at her. "We could send him someplace dark and sinister." He actually did a pretty good Peter Lorre.

I smiled at Ric. "How about someplace sunshiny and happy? That should drive him insane."

"Oh!" Barbara was at it again. "I had a wisp of an idea. Wait a minute, let me see if I can catch it." Silence fell while we tried not to stare at Barbara. I was about to nudge her to make sure she was awake when she said, "What if we sent him to the center of a sun?"

"What good would that do?" I asked.

"If we sent him to the center of a sun that's collapsing, I think it would be very difficult for him to escape."

"Barbara, you may just be brilliant!" Ric cried. "Time and space are distorted and gravity is immense. Eventually even light can't escape so how could he?"

"How do we find such a thing?" Cynthia asked.

"We go looking for it," Ric said.

"All of us?" asked Louise.

I nodded. "All of us."

"*No,*" Anna said, disgusted. "Make one *up*. We don't have to go anywhere."

"She's right," Rachel said, "And if we go out there, ditting around the universe, we are exposed and at risk."

"Even with the *Circle*?" Louise asked.

"Especially with the *Circle*," Rachel answered. "Because we don't know how to use it."

"Like not knowing how to use a gun and shooting yourself," Louise said.

"All right, it seems we're all agreed?" I got an affirmative from everyone. "We stay here and make one up. Anna, any ideas?"

Anna was bouncing with excitement. "I know how to make things because I've done it. I made Billy."

Rachel put a restraining hand on her head. "Slow down, quit bouncing and tell us that again. We're not sure we heard you right."

Anna managed to calm everything but her feet and they fidgeted like separate beings while she talked. "I made Billy. I wanted a pony and I thought and thought about it. I knew I wanted him to be black and white because I always wanted a black and white pony."

Ric stirred and I signaled him with my head not to interrupt.

"One day I thought about him so much, he was there."

"She visualized him so clearly, she made him manifest," Natalie said softly.

"Sounds grandiose," Ric smirked.

"That's what happened, though," Natalie said. "We've all worked with rearranging reality. What if we can do more?"

"What if we can create reality?" Rachel mused.

Natalie shrugged and pointed at Anna with her chin. "Obviously we can. No one told her she couldn't, so she just did it."

"That definitely seems to be the key," said Rachel.

"I think the first thing we need to do," I said as I poked the fire, "Is to be specific about what we want. Once we have that, we get in the *Circle* and see what scum we can call up. I *reeely* want to see his face when he realizes what's going to happen to him."

Ric whistled. "Ba-by! I do love a vindictive woman!"

I sneered. "I know better than that."

Ric shrugged, unmoved. "Shall I rephrase that? I like a vindictive woman."

"You are a vindictive woman," Natalie put in.

"Hag."

"It would help if we could rein in the silliness," Rachel said.

"Well!" Ric sniffed and flounced to a seat.

Barbara leaned forward. "What do we create for SoulJumper? I like the collapsing sun for a starter."

"Far, far away," said Cynthia.

"With an atmosphere so heavy he can't move," I said.

"In the final stages of collapse," said Natalie.

"With no light!" shouted Louise.

"It can't ever change. Then he could escape," Ric said.

"I think it would be nice if he couldn't hear anything," said Rachel.

We turned to Anna. "Your turn, honey," Rachel said. "What do you want for him?"

Anna looked solemn. "He has to watch us get free, over and over forever."

"Good, Anna! That should get him!" Rachel said.

"Shall we try?" I asked.

Barbara stood and reached a hand to pull Natalie from her chair. One by one, we stood and took our places in the *Circle*; Barbara, Ric, Natalie, Rachel, Anna, Louise, Cynthia, me and back to Barbara. We clasped hands and immediately the power coursed around the *Circle*, up through the center and out the roof. Then it did something new. Maybe because we were all of one mind, I don't know. Whatever, the ends of the spiral joined and formed an iridescent circle, whirling in our midst.

We never even had to say his name. Such is the *Maternal Circle of Power*. Our combined thought was enough to bring him there, to our center. He glared at us, unafraid. Suddenly, it was as if the house compressed and expanded. The huge plate glass windows exploded inward, showering us with pellets of safety glass. Hot wind blew through the broken windows so hard the drapes stood out from the walls. A foul miasma, greenish gray, rose from the floor and blew in our faces. Wherever we looked, it seemed the house was disintegrating around us. Beams fell from the ceiling and sheet rock began to peel from the walls and fall with a muffled *boom*.

"Don't let go!" Natalie cried. "Don't take your attention from the *Circle*!"

"You can't hurt us!" I looked into SoulJumper's eyes. Wrong move! Shouldn't have done that! Immediately I felt myself being sucked to the center of the *Circle*. To SoulJumper. My hands were slipping from Barbara's and Cynthia's! I heard Barbara scream, "Hold on, Cynthia!" With a wrench, I pulled myself back. *Don't go to his turf. Don't use* hatred to fight hatred, it'll never work. What then? I certainly didn't love the scuzzball!

But I did love my zhombie family. I could erect a wall of that love he could never climb because he couldn't comprehend it. I felt sad that he would go through eternity never knowing what it felt like to love and be loved.

He was going through eternity that way because I was going to see to it that he did.

I was going to lock him away where he could never get out.

In a collapsing sun.

Far, far away.

With an atmosphere so heavy, he couldn't move.

In the final stages of collapse.

With no light.

That would never change so he couldn't escape.

Where he couldn't hear anything.

And he had to watch us get free – forever.

The power whirled around SoulJumper and started to lift him up. I saw fear on his face as it dawned on him what was happening. I didn't feel exultant, I didn't feel vindictive, I didn't feel anything but the power, sweet and clean. It sang through us and made us glow from within.

The wind stopped. The house was still. SoulJumper screamed, long and hard. He whirled upward as the power separated and became a spiral again. Up and up, we heard SoulJumper screaming.

Then nothing.

A gentle breeze blew through the broken windows. Debris was everywhere. Chunks were missing from the roof. Still holding hands, we surveyed the damage.

"Look," Ric said, nodding with his chin.

We turned, holding on to each other tightly and looked through the shattered windows facing east.

The sun was rising, triumphant, over the Santa Lucias.

Chapter Twenty-Five

I couldn't help it, I started singing.

"Amazing Grace." Don't ask me why, it was primal. Everyone stared at me in surprise, then one by one joined in. We stood there in the middle of all that destruction, holding hands, singing to the rising sun. We only knew one verse, so we sang it over and over. Finally, we wound down.

"I wonder if the shower still works," Barbara said wistfully. The rest of us burst into laughter. "Well," Barbara huffed, "I just thought it would be nice."

"Barbara, my sweet Granny, I love you!" I gave her a big kiss on the cheek. "Don't you ever change! If it's a shower you want, a shower you shall have."

Ric said, "I used to have two."

"Actually, a shower does sound nice," Cynthia said.

"How do we do this without splitting up?" asked Rachel.

It seemed bathing was on the agenda. "Ric, you have a house in Big Sur that doesn't possess a hot tub? You got took, Bud," I prodded.

"I do *so* have a hot tub!" Ric said hotly. "On the deck outside the master bedroom!"

Natalie patted him soothingly. "There, there, dear. We all know you're a real estate wizard." She winked at me.

"Good thing," I said eyeballing what used to be the living room, "Cuz you're gonna need a new house."

"I vote hot tub," Barbara announced. "Enough chit-chat. Ric, how many bathing suits do you have?"

"Certainly not seven."

"If anybody's shy, they can wear their undies. Come on, let's go." Barbara herded us through the house.

We got around privacy issues by averting our eyes. It seemed odd, any of us being modest with what our other selves were occupied, at this very moment, doing. Maybe that increased our modesty. After a good soak, we took turns showering while the others crowded around, not looking. Actually, it worked quite well. The damage wasn't as bad in the back of the house and we had almost forgotten about it when we walked out, refreshed.

"Oooh," Barbara sighed.

Ric looked sad, then straightened his shoulders and said briskly, "Let's clear a place to sit down for now. It's a nice day, we don't have to worry about weather. I'll make some calls later to get this repaired. I've got a sneaking suspicion we don't have much time."

We all fell to clearing debris from chairs and loveseats. When the windows imploded, it blew hot ash from the fireplace everywhere, covering things with a fine gray powder and singeing some places.

"What the…?" I heard Louise say. She stared out the windows facing the ocean.

"What is it, Louise?" Cynthia asked.

"One of my other selves is here."

"What?" I asked.

"Where?" from Rachel.

Louise answered Rachel. "Just outside on the cliff. My first time line self is here."

Cynthia gasped, "Mine too!"

"I'm here too," cried Anna.

"Okay, folks, think fast. What do we do?" I hollered.

"I'm here too!" Natalie said. "My first time line!"

"That must be the one, then," Ric said, "The one she uses to access the *Circle*."

"I'm here now," I said grimly.

"We're all here," said Ric.

"What do we do?" Cynthia cried.

Barbara snapped to. "Everybody grab hold! Get in place!"

I glanced out the window and there, on the cliff's edge, I saw all of us. As if in a trance, I watched myself take Barbara's, then Cynthia's hands exactly as I was doing inside. Ric took Barbara's other hand and reached for Natalie's; a mirror image; one in the ruined living room, one on the towering cliff.

"What's going to happen?" Cynthia cried.

"We don't know!" I shouted. "Grab on, everyone!" It went on inexorably, hand grasping hand inside, outside, exactly alike, exactly at the same time. *Chink, chink, chink*, like links in a chain locking in, I could hear the hands making contact and holding. CLANG! With a sound like a metal gate closing, the last hand clasped. I didn't have to look outside to know the *Circle* was complete because I was in that *Circle*. I saw, with those eyes, what was manifesting at the center of that *Circle*.

A dark purplish/black cloud spun close to the ground. Thousands of eyes circled the vortex, gazing outward, searching for weakness and pain. Eyes of every color and description, eyes of victims wide open in anguish, seeking to ease their own torment by inflicting torment. I stared at it, aghast, from deep within my other self. I couldn't even look up to see if the others felt as I did, I could only stand and stare as the power within me gave this evil thing the energy to exist.

And to destroy me.

Inside the house, we were at the opposite end of the spectrum. The now familiar glowing galaxy swirled and then formed a ring. The light it emitted sparked in us and we glowed, golden.

Outside, the black cloud was draining us. I felt my other self slipping into it; feeding it; joining those eyes.

"Oh, no!" I thought. "You come home to mama." I called and cajoled and pulled. I'd been wanting to collect my other selves and now was as good a time as any to start.

Trouble was, it wasn't doing any good.

"You have no idea who I am!" Sharon's voice was a shrill roar inside my head.

Well, she was right about that. I didn't have much of an idea about anything. None of us did. Everything up till now had been dumb luck with a smidgen of cunning.

"I created you; it took me centuries and if you think I will let you go, you are sadly mistaken." Her voice was a cold hiss but so loud the noise of it in my head was making me cringe.

"Would you shut *up*?" Evidently it was bothering Louise too.

"Oh, brave little girl," came the sickening croon piercing my brain.

"Don't listen to her!" I shouted. "She's just trying to distract us! Call your other selves!"

Our *Circle*'s power moved among us and began to expand outward to the cliff's edge. Lustrous and gleaming, it surged like an immense wave. The black cloud boiled up to meet it. Then my other self was inside the purple/black cloud looking out. I could see the *Circle of Power*, only a short distance away but I couldn't reach it, couldn't move toward it. Things were flying around me in the darkness. Things I could sense and didn't want to see. Hands touched me out of nothing; hands that made my skin crawl. I heard the screams of tortured souls, souls long dead and unable to rest because they belonged to evil. There was a horrible wrenching noise.

We stood in the living room and looked at each other.

"Where did she take us?" Barbara asked.

"I don't know," I said. "I can't even find my other self."

"Anybody?" Barbara looked around the room at seven frightened faces. "No one?" Everyone shook their heads.

"I'm getting nothing," said Rachel.

"Can everybody sit where they are?" asked Ric, "I don't think we want to break up the *Circle*, do we?"

Everyone shook their heads, "No."

"Let's sit and try to think this out."

"I don't think we need to sit, I think we need to *do*!" Louise cried distractedly. "What if she takes our other selves? What if she can get the rest of us by having most of us?"

"Somewhat garbled but the sentiment is correct," Barbara said thoughtfully.

"Can we please *sit*?" Ric asked, exasperated.

"Of course, Ric, if it's so important to you," Natalie soothed.

"He shot her a dirty look. "Don't patronize me!" He plopped to the floor in a pout.

We all sat. We had to move a couple of chairs to keep the *Circle* intact but we managed it.

"Now what do we do?" quavered Anna.

"We find ourselves," I said.

Ric snickered. "You sound like a guru."

I eyeballed him. "You're certainly feeling better."

"Yes." Ric said smugly.

"What about this, y'all?" Barbara spoke up. "We don't know where she took our first time line selves. It may be she would love for us to waste energy chasing around looking for them What if Louise is right? If she controls most of us, she can eventually control all of us?"

"Where are you going with this, Barbara?" I asked.

"If she can, we can. We let the first time line go for now and gather up our other selves. Once we have them, we might be able to bring our first line back."

"Ions do it, why can't we?" quipped Louise.

"Right!" Barbara's eyes lit up. "What if it creates something like magnetic energy that naturally draws our other selves?"

Anna looked puzzled.

"Whoever holds the most cards wins, Anna," Louise said.

"Oh, I get it! You mean the more we have of us, the more we have of us!" Anna declared.

"Exactly," Barbara laughed. "Do you think you can get your other selves, Anna?"

Anna sobered. "I think so. They don't want to come, though."

"What do you mean?" Cynthia asked.

"I try," Anna told her, "They cry inside but they don't come."

"That's it in a nutshell," Barbara said, "How do we overcome control?"

"By not believing in it," Cynthia said. "That's how I learned to talk under control. SoulJumper told me I couldn't and I asked myself, *what if I can?*" She looked sheepish. "I have a lot of time on my hands at Anrica's.

"Good thing," I smiled, "We'll have to be sure and thank Anrica someday for not being there."

Ric stirred. "What if we all went together and got one of us at a time?"

"Sounds confusing," I grinned.

Rachel sang, "I love a parade…"

"Hey!" Ric snapped, "It was your idea we all traipse around together."

I glared at him.

"Okay, our idea. Whatever – don't you think it would work?" Ric whined.

"Actually, I do. I also think we're forgetting something again." Everyone looked at me. "We don't have to go anywhere. We call them to us."

"What do we do with them/us when we get them here?" Barbara asked.

"Ooo, glad you thought of *that*!" Ric said. "We'd have a plethora of ourselves!"

"Maybe the *Circle* will help," offered Natalie.

"What if we put whoever we're calling in the center?" Louise asked, "Then maybe the other self will be drawn in."

"And reunited," Cynthia smiled at her.

"I think it's definitely worth a try." Natalie stood and extended a hand to Ric. "Come on, you. Off your panties."

"Not to be mistaken with take off your panties," Ric said in a deep announcer's voice. He pulled on Natalie's arm making her stumble, then let go and hopped to his feet. Natalie popped him lightly on the back of the head with her open palm.

"Who's first?" Anna asked.

"Not to be mistaken with who's on first," Ric cracked.

We all turned and gave him a Look. He subsided, grumbling.

"How would you like to be first, Anna?" Barbara asked.

Anna beamed. "Sure!"

"You won't be scared?" Rachel asked.

"No." Anna answered simply.

"Let's do it," Louise said.

"Anna, where is your second time line self right now?" Natalie asked.

"In a house. With a man."

"What kind of house, Anna?" Natalie asked gently. "We need to know so we can get you out of there."

Suddenly, a much older woman looked out of Anna's green eyes. "I'm in a house in eighteenth century England. The man I'm with is an Earl. We are in a bedroom in a maroon canopied bed. The fire has burned low. The man will soon be asleep. I won't be there much longer."

"Okay." Natalie was all business. "In the center, Anna. Everyone, grab hold. Let's get this young lady out of there."

When our *Circle* was complete, the power spiraled around Anna and spun low. I bet it was beautiful in there! I concentrated on another Anna. I felt the power enter me, then fly outward. I actually saw the power enter a blue/green time line. I felt us all gather Anna tenderly in our arms and carry her away. Her little arms clasped around my neck. Then I was back in the *Circle* and there were two Annas in the center, staring at each other in awe. Anna reached out to Anna and they hugged, one Anna patting the other gently. And there was one. One Anna standing straighter and taller, pride shining from her face. One Anna, a step closer to being complete. We let the power cocoon her a little longer, just to make sure. We dropped our hands.

"Did it work, Anna?" Rachel asked.

"Um-hmm," Anna nodded shyly.

We all breathed a sigh of relief and shifted on our feet.

"Who's next?" Natalie asked briskly. Thank goodness for Natalie! We needed a diversion. None of us knew what to do with happiness anymore.

"How about Barbara?" Ric asked. "Age before beauty." Barbara made a face at him. "Careful it doesn't freeze like that," Ric smirked.

Barbara looked archly at Ric. "I'll go next if you're scared." She walked to the center and turned. "Ladies first and you said yourself you're not a lady."

"Well!" Ric huffed. "Look at the pot calling the kettle black!"

"I never understood that one," said Natalie, "But I assume you're saying Barbara's not a lady." She picked up Ric's hand. "I'm thinking it's a blessing none of us are ladies. Thanks to all of us doing things we were told not to, we may one day be free." Natalie looked purposefully at Barbara. "Where are you, Barbara?"

"This may be a little harder. I'm in the future, part of a group orgy at a sex club. We are, you might say, actively involved."

Ric started laughing. "This ought to mess with their heads!"

"Okay, *ladies*," I said, grinning around the *Circle* and taking Cynthia's and Ric's hands, "Let's go start some rumors!"

It was as before, except Barbara walked in and got Barbara. In front of a dozen astonished revelers, she pulled herself out of the pile and covered the other Barbara in a robe. She took her hand and led herself out of the room, closing the door gently behind them.

They were in the *Circle* with us clutched in each other's arms, shivering with emotion. Then one Barbara turned to us.

Arms outstretched, she spun for us to see. We dropped our hands.

"How does it feel, Barbara?" Rachel asked.

"*Amazing*. I didn't even realize I didn't feel whole!" She laughed. "Not my most eloquent statement but the best I can do under the circumstances."

"Ric?" Natalie poked him. "You're next in the *Circle*."

"I'm in Atlanta," he said walking to the center, "At the private home of a man and woman. Current day, affluent home. We are in a hot tub in a spa room at the back of their house." He cackled. "They definitely will not be getting their money's worth tonight."

We joined hands. The power built and we were in a steamy tile room. Three people stared at us from a hot tub. Ric and Natalie stepped forward and guided the other Ric from the hot tub, wrapping him in a towel. They disappeared in the steam and we were back in the *Circle* in Big Sur, two Rics within. One Ric grinned, the other smiled shyly. Hands reached out, touched and two Rics held each other close, then melded into one. He sighed.

We dropped our hands and Ric said quietly, Thank you." He held out his hands to Natalie and drew her to the center. "Your turn, Sis." He kissed her cheek gently. "Thank you."

"Anytime, Bro." She smiled at him, then glanced apologetically at Cynthia. "I'm with Anrica. In the south of France. A private home. There are several of us in a pleasure room."

Cynthia grimaced and shook her head. "That woman is so horny!" I squeezed her hand.

It should be good timing; everyone is actively engaged except me. My job is to watch right now."

Anrica's eyes almost bulged out of her head when she saw Cynthia. I imagine she ran straight to her phone to call and check on her 'property' as soon as we were gone. Take *that*, Missy! Even though 'her' Cynthia was still at home, she wouldn't be much longer. Not if I had my way.

The other Natalie looked up vacantly, then her eyes began to shine. This one knew exactly what was happening and she was ready. She threw a disdainful glance at Anrica and company, stood tall and gathered her robe around her. She walked forward proudly and stood next to the other Natalie.

Back in the living room, they searched each other's eyes, sighed and held each other. One Natalie stood tall in the center. She said, "Let's keep moving. Someone is bound to complain that their hookers are disappearing and we'll have all that to contend with as well." She smiled radiantly. "Thanks. I don't mean to seem ungrateful."

Rachel stepped forward. "We understand." She gave Natalie a quick hug and pointed her out of the *Circle*. "Now git. It's my turn."

"I'm in Spain. Not too far in the future, maybe twenty years. A private home, overlooking the Mediterranean. We are outside in a patio garden." She grinned devilishly. "Let's just say this man will not appreciate being interrupted. I, however, will enjoy it immensely."

We traveled but didn't travel with the power again. The time line was a bright flame blue. The john, a famous actor in current day, looked up in horror. He probably thought we were the press. The other Rachel saw us, smiled serenely, went to a fountain and washed her face. Water sparkling on her in the light we emitted made her appear to twinkle. She took the first Rachel's hand and we were back in the living room. Both Rachels smiled tenderly at Anna. Anna smiled back at one.

Each time I witnessed the reunion of selves, I saw my family members one by one become more whole. Each time a little prouder. I realized how much self-ownership meant. If we don't have ourselves, we have nothing.

"We already got your second time line, Anna," Rachel said, "So next is Louise. You ready, hon?"

Louise strode to the center. "I'm in Malibu. A home on a hill high above the ocean. Current day. There are four of us, three elderly men and me. We are in a swimming pool, which is on a knoll in front of the house. We will be breaking up a game of chase. It probably is a good thing. I think this guy is getting ready to have a heart attack!"

We laughed. Barbara said, "Let's definitely go save the old satyr's life!"

I don't think I'll ever get used to the beauty of the power. Different every time but the same, the color and intensity of the light it is made of are amazing.

Boy, Louise was right about this guy! Wheezing and coughing, he pursued Louise through shallow water. She eluded him easily. He snorted and fell. Avoiding grasping arms, Louise sensed us. Her head snapped around like a wild thing. She paraded out of that water, naked as a jaybird, looked the first Louise in the eye and nodded. In the living room, a puddle of water collected momentarily until two Louises grabbed each other in an exuberant hug, rocking back and forth. Then one Louise grinned and shrugged. "Sorry. I was in a hurry to get out of there."

"Show off!" snorted Ric.

"Hey, honey, if you got it, flaunt it," Louise said.

"That's right, you hag, rub it in," Ric said. He turned to Cynthia. "Next!"

"I'm on it!" Cynthia skipped to the center. "I'm in the future, a ship in space. We might have a little trouble finding it."

Ric harrumphed and Natalie elbowed him. Still, he had to erupt. "How many times have I found Rachel?"

"That's great, Ric. You can find this ship," Cynthia said firmly. "I'm in the captain's quarters, with the captain and his wife. Neither are humanoid. Be prepared, they resemble huge praying Mantises. Also a warning, they can be quite violent."

We entered a time line that was so dark blue it looked black. We had no trouble finding the ship, an odd looking thing resembling a partially worked wooden block puzzle. The captain's quarters were in the stern and took up three levels. Great, Cynthia, *where* in the captain's quarters?

Ah. A huge room with fantastic hammocks hanging. We took her out as one of the creatures twisted the soft skin of her stomach with its mandibles. Cynthia-in-the-hammock saw Cynthia-standing. She smacked the creature's head away from her belly as hard as she could and leapt to her feet. Crouched in a fighting stance and growling like a wild cat, she backed toward the *Circle*.

The Mantis-creatures snapped their jaws and milled around each other, not sure whether to attack or run. They chose neither. The first Cynthia bared her teeth and growled from the center and the second Cynthia growled and backed up. As soon as she entered the *Circle* we were back in Big Sur. We watched as one Cynthia raised from her crouch, turned and walked to the Cynthia in the center. Hands reached and one Cynthia stood smiling. "Okay, Mom! Last but not least!"

"Yes." We traded places. "I'm in the past. In Japan. A home near the sea, owned by a rich merchant. He is a regular client and books me for the entire night. He has just gone to sleep and I'm sitting outside his bedroom next to a pond, looking at the stars…Oops."

"What's oops, Lisa?"

"I'm not there anymore. I'm in a beauty parlor. From the looks of it, late 50's early 60's." I was silent, listening. "Southern accents. I wonder why I'm here?"

At that moment, a beautician spun the first chair around and I saw someone I hadn't seen before.

Sharon.

Complete with perm rods. Smacking gum, smoking an unfiltered cigarette.

"Fancy meetin' you here," she said dryly.

"I thought your 'do' was a little retro." It was the only thing I could think of!

Sharon smiled sourly. "You know what I don't like about you, Lisa? You think you're funny."

"I wasn't trying to be funny."

175

Sharon blew a cloud of smoke and studied me, smacking her gum.

Back in Big Sur, we were all watching. She knew it.

I stood in the middle of an ordinary, every-day small town beauty shop where a beautician was removing perm rods from Sharon's hair. The door opened and a woman in a poodle skirt came in on a rush of cool air. Must be winter, then, late 1950's. I looked at Sharon, frumpy white trash Sharon and waited for the axe to fall.

"You just tell them it won't work," she smacked, "I have an ace in the hole." Sharon ground her cigarette out and without looking at me, she said, "Now get your smart face out of here."

After that, my reunion of selves was a bit anticlimactic. When Sharon told me to leave, she cast me out and I was drawn into the *Circle* with ease. I must say, it was one of the more incredible things I've experienced. I do feel more whole…one step closer to home. It was as if an adored relative came back after a long absence. We did indulge in a moment of celebration – after all, each of us had retrieved our second time line selves.

Only three more to go!

Chapter Twenty-Six

"Y'all! Y'all!" Barbara called over the din. "Calm down! We need to talk!"

Laughing and woo-hooing and patting each other on the back, we found places to sit. I noticed Cynthia and Louise, arm around each other, laughing and sitting side by side. I thought, "That's sweet. At least some happiness will come out of all of this." I thought of Fleming. I'd never get over missing him. I sighed.

Barbara took my mind off self-pity with her first sentence. "Why was Sharon not concerned?"

I murmured, "What's this ace in the hole?"

"What, Lisa?" Ric asked. "Share it with all of us?"

I tittered. "You make it sound like I took Sharon's gum." What an image that evoked! *Yuck*. "No, I was just wondering what this ace in the hole is."

"Whatever it is, she's pretty sure of herself," Rachel said.

"Too sure," said Natalie. "You can bet it doesn't mean any good for us."

Louise shook her head. "It's hard to take her seriously when she looks like that."

"That's what she wants," Cynthia said.

Natalie spoke up. "Let's brainstorm. Maybe if we throw a bunch of ideas out, we'll hit on something worthwhile."

Ric looked at his watch and stood. "I need to call a contractor I know about repairing this damage." He nodded out to sea. "There's a storm out there and this has got to be protected from the weather."

"Where's the phone, Ric?" I asked.

"In the kitchen. That's the one I was going to use. Why?"

"It's probably futile," I shrugged, "Just worried about splitting up."

Ric smiled. "It's portable. I'll sit over by the fireplace and if you hens will keep the cackling down, I'll be able to hear." We all held our breath, figuratively, until Ric returned with his phone. "Luckily, I have this guy's number programmed into my phone. I don't have to go searching for it."

"Good thing," I remarked, "We'd-a looked really stupid traipsing all over the house behind you."

"Mom?" Cynthia stood next to me. I patted the floor and she sat. "Mom, have you talked to Dad lately?" I looked at Cynthia, surprised. "I mean," she said quickly, "Can you? Maybe he has some answers."

"I don't know, Cynthia. He died in the reality SoulJumper and Sharon put us in. He contacted me a couple of times." I sighed. "I was just thinking how much I missed him." I smiled at Cynthia forlornly. "He occupies a different world now."

"*Mom,* so do *you.*"

She was right. Of course SoulJumper had told me I couldn't reach Fleming. Ric said the bonds of love were strong enough to take you back if you knew what you were doing. It was too late for that, granted, but there were other ways Fleming might be able to help.

"We might be able to call him with the *Circle,*" Cynthia offered. "We could ask the others how they felt about it."

When Ric got off the phone, I ran it past everyone.

"We definitely could use some guidance," Rachel said.

"Yes but in all seriousness – no offense Lisa and Cynthia," Natalie looked at us, "How can Fleming help us? He doesn't know any more about our world than we do."

"Has anyone found their first time line?" Ric asked.

"No." from all of us.

"I don't like that, either," Ric mused. "I don't think that's Sharon's ace in the hole, though. I just don't like it that we can't even contact ourselves."

"It is eerie," Rachel said.

"Should we continue to collect ourselves?" Natalie asked.

"That's just it," Rachel fumed, "We don't *know*! We're operating completely in the dark."

"The way to hit your target in the dark," Anna said, "Is to make sure it's big." She stared at us with emerald green eyes and shrugged. "One of my uncles told me that."

Natalie laughed. "It has a certain amount of crazy logic."

"*We* certainly are a big target," Barbara said.

"Like the back side of an elephant," Ric quipped.

"No really," Barbara said, "We are like the proverbial bull in a china shop, crashing around the universe, drawing all kinds of attention."

"I think that's something we'll have plenty of leisure to worry about in the future." Everyone looked at me blankly. "Well? What are we going to do with ourselves once we're free? I imagine with all eternity at our disposal, we'll be able to perfect any nuances we overlook in the rush to survive. One thing we will have is time."

"Yeah," Louise said, "What we need to work on is our offense."

Cynthia said fondly, "Okay, coach. Play much football?"

Natalie looked at the two of them and raised an eyebrow at me. I nodded slightly with a tiny smile. Natalie beamed at our two young lovebirds. Love amid destruction. Life in the middle of death. A reminder that we could achieve some sort of, if not happiness, contentment in this state. As Cynthia and Louise giggled, momentarily caught up in each other, word traveled around the room. We all found a softer place in our hearts, watching those two. We needed it.

"Ahem." Barbara cleared her throat.

"It's okay, we choked up, too," I telegraphed with my eyes. She smiled.

"Louise is right, you know," Barbara said, "We've talked about this before, that we're always in a position of defending ourselves. We finally got angry and aggressive with SoulJumper. That worked."

"Sharon's a different ball of wax," Rachel said.

"Yeah," I nodded at Rachel, "Sharon told me SoulJumper was just a well paid executive."

Rachel shivered. "We don't have any idea how much power she has or how she can use it."

"You know what?" I blurted, "I'm getting the impression we make this up as we go along." Anna started to nod and fidget. I pointed at Anna. "That's right, isn't it? We create it?"

Anna was bouncing by now. "Uh-huh! We can make anything! I had fun making my house in France. You never saw my house. It was like one I read about in a book. I pictured it real hard and it was there!" She turned excitedly from one to the other of us.

"I bet it's still there," Ric said softly.

Anna heard him. "Oh yes! It's *real*. It's a cottage with a fireplace and a straw roof."

"We create more than things," I said flatly, "We create reality."

Silence.

"This is going to take some practice," Ric said glumly.

We cracked up. Ric glared at us, offended. "I'm *serious*. When I make jokes, you don't laugh. When I'm serious, you laugh. My feelings are hurt." Ric crossed his arms and pushed out his lower lip.

"We're sorry, Ric," I sputtered.

"Yeah," cackled Natalie, "We didn't mean to laugh."

"No, Ric," Barbara managed to choke out, "For some reason, it struck us as funny." Unfortunately, Barbara and I made eye contact after that last statement. It was all over. We shrieked with laughter while Ric fussed and pouted.

"It's true, you know," he raised his voice, "If everything we so much as think can manifest as reality, we need to learn to discipline our thoughts."

"Well said, brother!" Natalie thumped him on the back.

"You don't need to *burp* me," he snipped, "You need to listen to me for a change."

180

Natalie controlled her face and looked Ric in the eye. "We're listening."

"We know there are millions of realities," he stared sternly around the room, "We know time can be molded and shaped. The next step is to understand that everything" he looked at us from lowered brows "Everything we experience, we can control."

"Wow," said Louise. We all felt that way and took a moment to digest this information.

"That's big," Cynthia breathed.

"Schweetheart," Ric tipped an imaginary hat and winked, "That's what they all say."

Cynthia made a face at him. "*Now* he's trying to be funny."

"It is rather overwhelming," Barbara sighed.

"What a responsibility," Rachel said soberly.

"What is?" I spoke for all of us.

Rachel widened her eyes. "We are responsible for every single thing that happens to us. We control it. This could take centuries to perfect."

"We could start with making a place to send Sharon," said Louise. "I'd love to see that woman go down."

"We need to be careful," Natalie warned. "We might set off a reaction we're unprepared for."

"That's the sticker," I said, "Just how good is she?" I pointed at Ric. "*Don't* say it."

"I wasn't going to say anything!" He was the picture of injured innocence. We waited. "But I hear she has clients!"

"Huh?" Cynthia looked puzzled. "What's the punch line, Ric?"

He smirked. "Think about it. I don't care if the woman is immortal, that body is several hundred years old."

"Eeew!" squealed Anna.

"That's a mental image I could have lived without," said Barbara.

"Gross!" from Louise.

"Oh that's disgusting," I said.

Cynthia laughed. "What do you think her clients would do if they knew?"

"Same thing they'd do if they knew about us," I said sadly. "It's not pretty."

It seemed we all had our memories in this area, too. Everyone's eyes looked inward. We had common ground – we had all experienced that moment when we realized we were freaks and how society in any time, in any world, dealt with freaks.

Thank goodness we had each other.

I didn't think we could have bonded much tighter but we did at that moment. And woe be to anyone who tried to break that bond.

* * *

The wind was picking up, whistling through the broken windows. Clouds were visible in a low solid bank on the horizon.

"Ric, what did your buddy say about fixing this place?" I asked.

"He should be here any time with stuff to nail over the windows. He said he'd have to look at the roof, he might be able to nail down some plywood for now."

"In other words, it will be uninhabitable."

Ric nodded. "Seems so."

"Maybe we should rent a cabin. I have money, in accounts in Monterey."

"For that matter, I have too. I have plastic," he announced. "We probably won't be able to see out until they get the glass for the windows, so we may as well go someplace else. A house without a view in Big Sur just isn't a house!"

"Spoken like a true realtor," I said dryly. "Got a phone book? We'll call around and see who's got a vacancy."

The cheapest place we could find was $350.00 a night. Ric shrugged. "That's why I bought here. I figured I may as well get some return on my money eventually." He grinned. "Go ahead. I told you antiques have been good to me. I'll pick up the tab."

"I'll say they've been good to you! If I'd known you had that kind of money, I'd have married you long ago!"

"Who's talking about marriage?" Rachel detached herself from the others and joined us by the fireplace.

"Me," I said, "Old moneybags here – he could support me in the style I'm unaccustomed to!"

Rachel laughed. "Champagne tastes on a beer budget, Lisa?" She eyeballed Ric. "Wouldn't it be illegal for you guys to marry? Aren't you a little too closely related?"

Ric snorted. "Not a match made in heaven."

"A marriage of convenience?" I wheedled.

"Why, Lisa," Ric smiled an oily smile, "I never realized what a little money grubber you are. I find that attractive in a woman."

"Pick on somebody your own size, greaseball," I growled. "Okay, everybody!" I clapped my hands. "Gather your belongings and anything of Ric's you want to take."

"Hey!" Ric squeaked.

"Mr. Moneybags here is putting us up in a deluxe cabin with a view in Big Sur," I announced, "Gather up your pantaloons, girls, we're going on an outing!"

Naturally, we didn't have much to pack. It wasn't long before we were standing outside, watching Ric back a gigantic black SUV out of the garage. "True to form," I remarked, "Got this huge atrocity he can't drive on ninety percent of the roads down here. Some people got all the money in the world and still can't buy a lick of sense."

"At least it has room for all of us!" Ric yelled, muffled from inside the car. "Snipe all you want but at least no one's walking!"

"That's true, Ric," I said, "But you drive this tuna boat slowly."

"Yeah, yeah, yeah," came from the driver's seat. "Little old lady afraid to ride with the big bad wolf?"

"Where are the fold-down stairs? I swear, you need a step ladder to get in this thing."

It was tight, even in Ric's monster vehicle but we made it. Fifteen minutes later, we pulled in a tiny resort dripping from the cliffs. It appeared to have been built in about 1950 and not upgraded since.

"*This* is $350.00 a night," Natalie said flatly.

Ric hopped out and started opening doors. "Yep. Welcome to Big Sur!" he said cheerfully, "Be sure and bring your wallet!"

"And go home when it's empty," I put in.

The wind was practically lifting us off our feet. Louise stood leaning into the wind like a sailboat with her short hair blowing back, surveying the coast. "It sure is pretty."

"You're right, Louise, it is," I said, grabbing what bags we had. "Ric and I are just being cynical. There is truly no place like it in the world."

We got checked in and decided the rates weren't so bad after all when we discovered our cabin had three bedrooms and a kitchenette. The décor was eclectic but it was roomy. We had a nice partial view of the Pacific from the living room windows, so Ric was content.

"Oh look!" Natalie cried, "There's a trail down the cliffs to a private beach!"

"Down the cliff is fine," Ric said, "It's coming back up that's the killer."

"Like it matters to you."

"Well, that's what everyone *says*," Ric whined.

"Will you two ever grow up?" Louise asked.

"I certainly hope not!" Ric flashed back.

Rachel laughed. "Me too, Ric."

"Whaddoyamean?" Ric asked, suspicious.

"Nothing." Rachel batted her eyes at him. "I just don't want you to change."

"Mmf." Ric grumped. He looked at all of us standing around wondering what to do with ourselves. "Why's everybody staring at me? Sit! Sit!" He waved his arms at us.

There were straight-backed chairs and lawn chairs and even a wicker armchair. A twin bed doubled as a couch; Cynthia and Louise sprawled there. Barbara took the wicker armchair and we divvied up the remaining chairs, with Anna ending up cross-legged on the floor. Without even realizing it, we had seated ourselves in the order of the *Circle*.

"Not bad," Ric approved.

Barbara looked around "We do seem to be getting in the habit. That's good."

"Self-preservation is healthy for you," cracked Cynthia.

I smiled at her. "That needs to be our motto. I've been thinking…"

"Uh-oh," said Ric.

I refused to be distracted. "Okay. Say we can create reality." Everyone groaned. "I understand this is a new concept we're into here and not a simple one but bear with me. What if we are able to create a reality in which we aren't under bondage? If we do that, how will Sharon fight it?"

"This is gonna take some heavy believing," Louise said.

"Yes," said Barbara, "From all of us. We have to believe in it so much that we make it exist. And not just in one time line, either. In all five we can walk."

"What if we did it from the sixth?" Ric asked.

"I don't know," Natalie said, "Do we have time to take on a sixth line? None of us has been there, right?"

A chorus of "No," all around.

Barbara shook her head. "I don't think we ought to be charting two new territories at once."

"The question is, do we need it right now, or can it wait?" I asked. "To me, it seems like it would add another degree of

185

difficulty. We'd have to worry about six time lines instead of five when we create an alternate reality."

"Will those five time lines keep going once we create the new one?" Cynthia asked.

"Yes," I nodded, "But without us. When we create the alternate reality, we have to concentrate on having all our selves together. We'll pull ourselves out of all those time lines at once, into the new reality."

"That would be a quicker way than gathering them one at a time," Barbara said.

"Whoa, whoa, wait a minute," Rachel said, "Just how do we go about creating this alternate reality?"

I looked at Anna. "Want to tell her?"

"We decide how we want it to be, then think about it real hard, right?"

I nodded. "We have to be one mind with only one thought. No discrepancies."

"No *doubts*." Ric glared at Rachel.

"No *problem*." She glared back.

"Good," said Natalie, "We're clear on that. What about our alternate reality? It should be in the current time, right?"

Silence. None of us knew what to say. Except Anna. "First where, then when, then what."

"Child, you are a gold mine of information!" exclaimed Barbara.

The older woman looked out of Anna's eyes again. "I've had lots of years to work on it."

"I apologize Anna," Barbara was contrite. "I shouldn't…"

"It's okay," Anna smiled, "I can't blame you for treating me like I'm eight when I look eight." She paused. "Sometimes it's easier to be eight."

"Yes," said Barbara, "I can imagine. So first 'where'. How about here?"

"We could create a reality where my house is fixed," Ric said.

Natalie frowned. "Don't be frivolous."

"I'm not!" Ric cried hotly. "It would give us a place to be!"

"It would also give us more to visualize," I said, "Let's stick with what we can see."

"Good idea," said Barbara, "So 'where' is here. Next is 'when'. Current time. Now 'what'."

"How about a reality where Sharon doesn't exist?" Louise asked.

"No." I shook my head. "That's letting her off easy. The woman has to be punished."

"O-kay!" Ric looked me over warily. "Remind me not ever to get on your bad side!"

"I'm sorry if I seem vindictive," I said, not sorry at all, "I don't think she ought to be able to get off free as a bird after what she's done."

"I agree," said Barbara.

"Me too!" cried Anna.

"I think she should have to live with herself," Cynthia said.

"With a constant reminder of why she's there," said Natalie.

"Okay, okay!" Ric held up his hands. "But can we free ourselves first?"

"*What* is the hard one," Anna said.

"It is," Natalie agreed. "We know we want a reality where all our selves are reunited and not under bondage."

"That's a good start, Natalie," Barbara said, "Anyone got anything else to add?"

"She's pretty much covered it," I said.

"This seems entirely too simple," Rachel said nervously, "Shouldn't it be harder?"

"The hard part is within us," Barbara said. "We cannot have any doubt that we can do this or it won't happen."

"Um…not to throw a monkey wrench into the works or anything…" Ric said, "Has anyone had contact with their first time line?"

"No," we all answered.

"Will we be able to pull the first line back as well?"

I looked at Ric. "We'll have to be able to."

He nodded. "Ah.'k. Just wondered."

"This is still spooking me," said Rachel, "It's too easy. Where's Sharon? You know she knows we're doing this!"

"Will you *stop*?" Ric cried, exasperated. "You're going to call her here!"

"Oh, I've been here for a while," came from the kitchenette.

Chapter Twenty-Seven

That Sharon woman sure had a knack for startling us! She came in the living room smiling like a crocodile. "You guys keep providing me with entertainment." She pulled out a cigarette and lit it. "The only thing that makes me mad," she blew smoke out the side of her mouth, "Is the amount of money you're costing me."

"Poor baby," Cynthia muttered.

Sharon shifted her blank gaze to Cynthia. "You got a smart mouth just like your mother," she said idly, "I think it's time you left."

And Cynthia was gone! Just like that! No snapping fingers, wiggling of the nose, just *gone*. We stood frozen in horror. Louise cried, "Cynthia!"

Sharon laughed and pointed at her with her cigarette. "Poor baby!" she mocked. "I'm telling all of you for the last time. Give it up. I'm getting tired of this little rebellion of yours." Then she was gone, too.

"All right everyone!" I snapped, "Grab hands! Let's find Cynthia!" The power swirled, then spread out, searching. We reached with our minds trying to find any hint of Cynthia. I called to the child I was never allowed to bear. I felt the power surge through me and wash me clean of all emotion, leaving only intent.

We entered a green time line.

Standing on a deserted beach, we gazed around blankly. Rachel screamed and pointed out to sea. Coming at us with a roar like a thousand freight trains was a tsunami. We looked up and up to barely be able to see the crest. Before we could move, it had hit us, ripping the *Circle* asunder. I was swept into the immense wave and carried along, tumbling, in its momentum. I wasn't worried about drowning but I was worried about being buried, technically alive, under tons of mud and water.

"Well, Lisa, what if it weren't real?" a voice said inside my head. "What if you were standing on the beach with the others and there was no tsunami?" I was on the right track but it was hard to think when being carried in the center of a tsunami to goodness knows where. Hopefully, we wouldn't smack up against anything soon. I could feel the weight of the water, trying its best to crush me. "The beach. The beach. No tsunami. The beach."

Oh! I *did* it! The others weren't there though. Yet. I started calling them out loud. What the heck. I didn't think there was anyone who could hear me. I shouted to them to visualize the beach, come back to the beach. I felt Barbara's hand take mine and her voice joined in calling, calling.

Slowly we got everyone reassembled. Everyone but Cynthia.

"This was a trap," I said.

"I didn't know she could do that," Ric said shakily.

"She must have put an alternate Cynthia here," Natalie said, "Then snatched her when we got here."

"Now we know," I said.

"Let's go back to Big Sur and try again," Rachel said belligerently. We looked at her, surprised. "I'm getting real sick of that woman."

"Good for you, Rachel!" Ric cried. "Back to Big Sur it is!"

I couldn't believe how happy I was to see that seedy little rental cabin. I shuddered whenever I thought of being trapped in all that water. Sharon had probably created a world where that tsunami went on forever, intended to carry us along endlessly.

But it hadn't. Why was that?

I'd worry about that later. Cynthia was more important. I met Barbara's eyes. Hers had a steely look to them. For that matter, so did everyone's.

I imagined Cynthia laughing on the floor of Ric's living room with Louise and Anna. I thought of Louise's budding love for her and wanted, more than anything, for my daughter to experience that love.

"Bring her here this time," Ric shouted, "Don't go anywhere!"

The power swirled up and up, then compressed into a circle. As it swirled, it changed colors, green to blue to lavender to pink to gold and back to green. Natalie began to call Cynthia's name. Soon we all were. "I love you, Cynthia!" I cried, not meaning to. Barbara squeezed my hand, understanding.

Then a form appeared in the center of the *Circle*. "Cynthia!" yelled Louise. It was Cynthia! I couldn't quite see her face…

"Cynthia!" I called desperately.

"*Cynthia*," mimicked Sharon snidely, her face on Cynthia's body. "Cynthia, come back!"

Unnerved, I dropped Barbara's and Louise's hands and the *Circle* was broken. "Someone want to explain how she managed to do that?" I asked.

"I suggest we talk about this a bit before we try again," Barbara said.

"That might be wise," said Natalie.

We all sat, maintaining the order of the *Circle*.

"She's using our power against us," Rachel said. "Somehow, she's taking the power we generate and using it."

"You know," I said, "When I was a kid, we had this chant; *the game is locked, the game is locked and nobody has the key*."

"Yes, Lisa?" Ric raised an eyebrow. "There's a point to this story?"

"Its intention was that no one could join the game after we had said that chant."

Barbara got a speculative look. "What if we could lock her out?"

I nodded. "Maybe she's letting us do all this stuff because she draws energy from the *Maternal Circle of Power* every time we create it."

"That would certainly explain a lot," Natalie said.

"Oh, yeah," said Ric, "If she draws power every time we use the *Circle*, she sure ain't gonna get mad at us for using it!"

"She might actually create reasons for us to use it," Rachel said.

"Yeah, like snatching Cynthia," Ric said.

"We have to get her back!" I cried desperately.

"We will." Barbara patted my knee. "We'll find a way."

"Maybe we could lock Sharon out," Anna said.

"How?" asked Rachel.

Anna shrugged. "I don't know. Create the *Circle* and don't let her in."

"I wonder if we can marshal the power somehow," Rachel said. "Every time we create the *Circle*, we just do it without any thought of controlling it. What if we created it and kept the power in one place?" Rachel looked bemused. "Am I making any sense?"

"The secret to any power is control," Natalie said.

"Right!" Rachel said, "And we don't have any. So far, we go along for the ride, we don't drive."

"So, the idea is, we need to be more specific." Barbara shook her head. "I feel so ignorant!"

"Speaking for all of us," Ric said. "We all feel ignorant."

"Only because we are," I said morosely.

"Why don't we try locking her out?" asked Anna. "We could make the *Circle* and just say she can't come in."

Rachel answered her, "It's worth a try. Should we go after Cynthia, too?"

"Yes." Natalie spoke for Louise and I. "But first we make the *Circle* and lock Sharon out. Should it be an explicit thought? Like, 'We're making this *Circle* and we're locking her out'?"

"We'll go with yes as none of us knows," I said. "I would imagine the more precise, the better."

"Let's do it, girls," Ric said positively. His attitude galvanized all of us. We stood and clasped hands.

I envisioned the *Circle* forming a wall and keeping Sharon away. Not even a crack, where the tiniest bit of energy could creep out. This power did not belong to her; she had no right to it. I would no longer allow her to steal the only birthright we had left.

Oh, it was different already. "We probably should have been doing this all along," I thought. The spiral was more compact, staying within the confines of the *Circle* instead of going high above us, then dropping. When it circled, it entered us rather than whirling in the center. Now this was power!

I concentrated on keeping the power with us and called Cynthia. It only took a minute. Cynthia was sitting cross-legged on the floor in front of us. She looked up in delighted surprise.

We were careful with the power when we broke the *Circle*, too, this time. We held it in us when we let our hands go. No more scattering it carelessly throughout the universe.

Cynthia jumped up and started hugging with me. "I'm so happy to see y'all! I couldn't even feel anyone any more. She sold me! To some guy in the future! For *good*, just went off and left me there!" She got to Louise and gave her a rousing kiss on the lips. "I promised myself if I ever saw you again, I was going to do that!" Louise looked pleased and flustered as we laughed.

"We have a lot to tell you, Cynthia," I said, "Things we learned about the *Circle*."

"Could we tell her outside?" Natalie pleaded. "The wind died and the sun's getting ready to set. I'd love to watch it."

We looked at each other. "I can't see where it makes any difference," I said. "Being inside only gives us the illusion of safety." We trooped out and found a place on the cliff where

193

we could all sit and watch the sunset. It was nice out. "Good idea, Natalie." I smiled at her.

She beamed ecstatically. "It is so beautiful here!"

We took a moment to enjoy the sun's last light reflecting on the storm clouds still hovering on the horizon. High above the water, it seemed we could see halfway around the world. A last big set of waves came in and crashed on the rocks below.

"It sure is nice not to be in that water," I said.

"What?" Cynthia asked.

We took turns and by the time the sun had set, we had told Cynthia about everything that had happened to us. We wandered into the cabin in the gathering night, discussing the difference in the *Circle* this last time.

"As far as you know, she didn't pick up on it?" Cynthia asked.

"As far as we know," Barbara answered. "Of course, we can't be sure, she could be setting us up again."

We went in the cabin's living room and sat in the *Circle*. It really was becoming automatic.

"I propose we think positive," Cynthia announced.

"We'll try." Natalie smiled bitterly.

Ric stood. "I think we need a coffee break. In every sense of the word."

Rachel looked up at him. "Ric, we can't afford to take a break right now."

Ric bounced into the kitchenette, tossing airily over his shoulder, "I think we need a mini-vacay. We should forget all our troubles for at least twenty minutes. I'll be right back."

We all stared at Natalie. "Don't look at me!" Natalie shrugged. "I've never been able to do anything with him!"

"Maybe he's right," I said, "Sometimes when you let everything go, your best ideas come to you."

Barbara stretched. "All right then, we'll take our chances." She turned to Louise. "Tell a little about yourself, honey."

"Don't you *dare* start without me!" Ric hollered from the kitchenette. "Give me five more minutes!"

I should have known Ric would come prepared. I went in the kitchenette to help and Ric had a goodie box he was unloading, coffee already on. "For someone who can't taste anything, you sure enjoy food," I remarked.

Ric stopped opening containers and watched the coffee drip into the pot with a dreamy expression. "It's the memory of the enjoyment that went along with food that keeps me doing it. There's a companionship in sharing food; I keep trying to re-create it."

"I understand," I said softly, "Fleming and I used to enjoy our meals so much."

Ric turned to me. "You really miss him, don't you?"

"Every minute of every day." I looked at Ric bleakly. "He was my other half. I honestly feel like I'm less of a person without him."

Ric handed me a tray full of goodies and picked up one loaded with coffee and cups. He kissed me on the cheek as he edged past me in the tiny kitchenette, balancing china. His eyes were filled with sadness when they met mine. "I know. Believe me, I know. And unfortunately, it doesn't fade with time."

Touché, Sharon.

Chapter Twenty-Eight

By the time I made it to the living room, Ric was pouring coffee. "Now Louise," he smiled like a TV hostess, "Tell us about yourself."

Barbara giggled. "You remind me of me!"

I handed around goodies. "You know, when we have time, we should explore our relationship to each other."

"That's a wonderful idea, we could draw up a family tree," Barbara said, "For now, though, let's hear about Louise."

Louise looked embarrassed. "There's not much to tell. I was born in Indianapolis, Indiana and lived there until I was taken."

"When was that?" asked Natalie.

"My sixteenth birthday," Louise sighed. "My Mom and Dad think I was burned up in a car wreck. I guess that's better than the truth."

"We can't answer that one," I said. "I've asked myself *what if?* so many times. And there are so many *what ifs* in existence; all the alternative realities. Somehow, SoulJumper and Sharon put us on an endless loop."

"You know," Ric mused over his coffee cup, "We must be doing something right. He stayed put."

"That's true," said Natalie.

"So far, so good," said Rachel. We looked at each other, scared to feel too successful but wanting to, all the same.

Barbara leaned forward and took a cookie. Her and her infinitesimal bites! I could learn a thing or two. Barbara dabbed her lips with a cheap paper napkin as if it was made of the finest linen. "Rachel, where are you from?"

"I'm from New Orleans."

"*No!*" Barbara said, delighted. "I'm from Slidell!"

"I know. My mama used to have an old, old photograph of you. It was taken before you disappeared." Rachel smiled. "You were so young and beautiful."

"Oh my gosh," breathed Barbara, "It stands to reason that someone from my family would have stayed in the area and managed to hang on to a few things." She thought for a second. "It never dawned on me…" She looked up with a bright smile. "It's an odd feeling."

"One most people don't experience," I said.

"Go on, Rachel," Natalie urged.

"Well, I was born out of wedlock and my mama took her mama's maiden name and gave it to me, too."

"So you're a Sheridan?" Barbara cried.

Rachel nodded. "Somehow mama gave me a normal life. Aside from the teasing of the other kids. I went to secretarial school and was twenty-three and had just landed a good job when I was taken. People think I was murdered walking home from work one evening."

"There's more, isn't there, Rachel?" Barbara asked gently.

Rachel sighed. "Yes. I had met the nicest young man. He was walking me home that night; he got blamed for killing me. With no body, he wasn't convicted but he still lives with the suspicion."

"SoulJumper and Sharon have a lot to answer for," I said grimly.

Natalie said, "I had just married. I was only twenty. I was so in love. Guillaume was a sculptor, dark and exciting. We lived in New York and I promoted his work to galleries. We were a good team and had already had some success. He thinks I was abducted."

"Did you live in New York, too, Ric?" I asked.

"Yes. Not too far from Natalie and Guillaume. My partner, Michael and I had a wonderful apartment. I sold exclusive women's clothing during the day and we danced all night. I was in heaven! He thinks I dropped everything and left him without a word. It still breaks my heart."

"My Mama thinks I fell in the river and froze to death," said Anna.

"I had an accident on horseback," Cynthia said. "Traveler came home without me one day."

"I was bitten by a black widow," I said, "Only they took Fleming from me rather than taking me out of my life."

"Wonder why they changed it when they got to you?" Natalie asked.

"Probably because they could," I answered.

Barbara stirred. "Lisa, didn't Fleming tell you about us taking on another time line?"

"That's right, he did! I forgot all about that!" I explained to the others about hearing Fleming's voice saying "another time line. That's when Barbara and I took on another time line. We wouldn't have thought of it without him."

"Interesting," said Ric.

"Maybe he can help us!" cried Cynthia.

"Should we call him?" Rachel asked.

I tried not to appear too eager. We all looked at Natalie. "I know, I said not to call him. I was misinformed." She grinned. "I say aye!"

"I say I?" Louise asked. "What does that mean?"

Rachel smiled. "She means yes. The second 'I' is a-y-e."

"Oh! Then I say aye!"

Rachel stood. "Aye."

Anna popped up. "Aye!"

"We can stop with the 'aye'. I think we're all agreed." Ric stood. "We call Fleming and ask him…what?"

"Um- what to do about Sharon?" Barbara stood, pulling me to my feet.

"How about how to protect ourselves from Sharon?" I grabbed Cynthia's hand.

Louise said, "I'd still like to rearrange her face."

"Hold that thought," Ric said, "We may need it later. Cynthia, you clear on how we did the *Circle* last time? Lock

Sharon out and keep the power in us, don't let it go everywhere."

Cynthia nodded, brown eyes huge. She looked at me. I said, "Let's call your Dad."

Cynthia gulped, then took a deep breath. "Let's call Dad."

I could feel Cynthia's amazement when the power entered us. It was as if a blockage had been removed and now we received the full force of the power. I must confess it raised the hair on the back of my neck. Overwhelming or not, the power was ours. Totally.

We called Fleming. At first he looked like a watercolor left out in the rain. Then he began to solidify and soon he stood before us as real as he had been in life. I was so glad to see him, all I could do was stare.

Fleming said, "It's about time y'all learned you could do that! I've been waiting. I was hovering around," he grinned at me, "But I couldn't do much. Frustrating!"

"Fleming, it's so good to see you!" I said. "Can I hug you?"

"Oh yes." He suited action to answer. "I'm as solid and three dimensional as you. I've been trying to get through to you since shortly after the Okanogan episode."

"I'm so sorry, Fleming."

He smiled at me sweetly. "Honey, we've both learned a lot. We had to start somewhere. I had my own preconceived notions to contend with. When all this is over, maybe we can get caught up."

"You've been aware of what's happened?" asked Natalie.

Fleming nodded and put his arm around me. "I haven't been far from this one since I discovered I could do it." Fleming looked warmly at Cynthia. "Hello, Cynthia."

She grinned shyly. "Hi, Dad."

"Dad-but-not-Dad, huh?" he asked softly.

She nodded. "But I think I can handle it."

"Good." Fleming had me formally introduce him to everyone. Even though he'd been watching and felt like he knew them, no one really knew Fleming. We found another chair in one of the bedrooms and sat, us in the *Circle*, Fleming slightly outside it. When I tried to pull his chair forward, he shook his head. "No. I'm not part of the *Maternal Circle of Power*. I'll only weaken it if I try to join in."

Ric cleared his throat. "So, Fleming, the Big Question. What's it like?"

Fleming laughed. "Death? What do you guys care? You're immortal."

"Oh come on, Fleming," Natalie cried, "It's the oldest question in the universe!"

"It's just what you make it. Just like life." Fleming paused. "Minus the body, of course."

"Not that different from our world?" I asked.

"Some ways yes, some ways no."

"You're being very obscure," Barbara observed.

"Sorry," Fleming chuckled, "It's an obscure subject."

"So, Fleming, do you think we're on the right track? If we don't believe in our bondage, it doesn't exist?"

"Yes, I do. It's not quite that simple but yes." He nodded around.

"What about Sharon?" Louise asked, "What if we don't believe in her?"

"No, I'm afraid not," Fleming answered. "You'll probably have to devise some sort of confinement for her. You can't just not believe in an entity that's been around as long as she has." He thought for a second. "I'm not sure entities are something that's fluid. Events, however, are. Physical form is fluid, time is fluid, light is fluid – y'all already know this."

"Yes but it's good hearing it from somebody else," Natalie said.

"Well, what if we created something for Sharon the way we did for SoulJumper?" Rachel asked.

"Maybe if we take care of her, the other stuff will disappear," Cynthia offered hopefully.

"I doubt it." I looked at Fleming. "Because we have to take care of it. Am I right?"

"As far as I can tell. If you just take care of her, the time lines of you in bondage would go on. You have to stop them. Once that's done and you get yourselves back together, you should be strong enough to fight Sharon." Fleming looked solemn. "Because that's what it's going to be."

"This not believing – that's not all there is to it, right?" Ric asked.

Fleming smiled. "No. The worlds Sharon and SoulJumper have created are not going to politely disappear for you. You have to take yourselves out of whatever time line they're in, bring them back and keep them here. They will try to return because it's the only thing they know. You have to hold them with you until you can become one again." He chuckled. "You're going to have a bunch of strangers in a very small house!"

"We each have three more time lines," Ric said, "Do we have to collect them one at a time?"

"I honestly don't know, Ric," Fleming answered, "I would think it should be possible to gather them all at once. Same way you did before but reaching for all your selves instead of one."

"This is sounding complicated," said Louise.

"Yes," Fleming said.

"In other words, it is complicated," said Natalie.

"No more so than what we've already done," Rachel said, "If you think about it, we've already covered the basics. We knew it would take a long time to perfect."

"But we don't have time!" Louise cried, "I'm sick of her controlling any part of me!"

"Louise is right," I said, "We don't have time."

"No but you do have the *Circle*," Fleming said, "That makes up for a lot."

"We've been lucky so far," I said.

"Not just lucky." Fleming shook a finger at me.

"Let's not forget this ace in the hole she claims to have," Ric said, "She seemed awfully confident."

"You don't think it was latching onto the power of the *Circle*?" Natalie asked.

"No, it has something to do with the *Circle* itself," Ric said absently.

"Could she have another one?" I asked.

"Possible," Ric answered, "Remember she used our first time line selves against us. We still can't find that line."

Fleming said, "Yes but she should know there's always a chance you could reunite your selves. I don't think she would risk everything on that if it were an issue. It has to be something so fundamental that she can stop the whole shootin' match with it." He thought. "I don't understand it yet. Maybe you guys should reunite your selves and see what kind of reaction that sparks."

"We've been on the receiving end of her reactions often enough," I said dryly.

"Well," Fleming shrugged, "At least you'd be expecting this one."

"Look, we know we're not going to get through this without bumping heads with Sharon," Ric said, "I say let's go ahead. Don't let fear of the consequences stop us."

"It never did before," I mumbled.

"That's just it!" Ric cried. "Look how much we've accomplished. We couldn't have done it if we were scared of how Sharon would react."

"True," I said. I looked around the *Circle*. Willing faces, all. "Okay, then. Ric's right. Let's go ahead."

Fleming stood. "I'm going over here so I'll be out of the way. If I can assist at all, let me know. I'll be on watch." He stationed himself by the front door.

We began clasping hands, one by one, stating our intent with each handclasp.

"We will reunite our selves," from me.

"We will end our bondage," from Barbara.

"We will find our first time line selves," Ric said as he clasped in.

"We will belong to no one but ourselves," Natalie said.

Then Rachel, "We will allow no one to steal our power."

"We will be free," Anna said.

"We will lock Sharon out," said Louise.

"We will defeat Sharon," Cynthia said firmly.

The *Circle* was complete. I wondered what Fleming thought, really seeing it for the first time. Then I was too busy to think much of anything.

We were in all the time lines at once. Eight of us, three time lines each, twenty-four, total. Past, future, current day; private homes, brothels, palaces, mansions, spas; we were in them all. We found our first time line selves. Sharon had buried us deep in a limestone cavern. Her property on Pico Blanco was dotted with them. We were at the bottom of the deepest one, covered with tons of dirt and rock. We collected ourselves in every stage of undress and every manner of sexual act.

We brought them all home.

We stood in our *Circle*, light flashing from the walls of the cabin and brought each and every part of ourselves back where they belonged. Slowly but surely, we became whole.

Slowly but surely, we took back the legacy that had been stolen from us.

Chapter Twenty-Nine

At first, it was mass pandemonium inside me. Divergent selves, each possessing individuality and life of its own, together. Fleming was right, this would take some doing! I glanced around and froze. The beauty I saw calmed the din inside me. I wondered if I had the same expression of awe I saw on everyone else. And if I was surrounded by the same golden light. I could see impressions of other selves around Cynthia; mirror images that appeared to float. Oh! Everyone else had them, too, so I must. I concentrated on bringing the images into myself. For a moment, it was like living in a dormitory. Then pieces started sliding in place. I felt like I was focusing a very large camera.

The images and golden glow were fading. We must be nearing the end of the process. I just knew I had never, ever felt like this before.

When we broke the *Circle*, the energy that we kept solidified all my selves. I knew I would have work to do, keeping it all together but – hey – I could take that as it came. For now I felt wonderful.

I turned to Fleming. "We did it."

"Yes, my love, you did."

Cynthia grabbed me in an exuberant hug. Louise joined in, adding a hop. Soon we were all hopping and hugging. Everyone was talking at once, comparing notes. I pulled Fleming into the happy melee. Everyone was thanking him. "I do have the benefit of some guidance," he said modestly, "You guys don't."

Fleming detached me from the horde and took me in the kitchenette. He looked so sad I blurted out, "Fleming what's wrong?"

"I have to go now."

I was silent for a second. "I see." I touched his face gently. "For good?"

"I don't know, sweetie. We have a shared destiny, even though SoulJumper and Sharon distorted it. That's why I was able to come help you." He shifted on his feet. "Now that you're all back together," he grinned, "You don't need me."

"Yes I do," I cried, "I do need you!"

"That's what I meant by a shared destiny. We were supposed to have spent eternity together. We have to learn to live with the eternity we've got. I have places to go that you can't go now."

"Fleming…"

"Call if you need me." He pulled me close and held me, kissing my hair. "And when you do put Sharon away…"

"Yes, my love?" I murmured into his shirt. At least he didn't have to worry about me crying all over him any more.

I felt Fleming's arms tighten momentarily. "Get in a punch for me."

"I will."

Fleming pulled back and looked in my eyes. "I love you. I always will."

"We truly were a match made in heaven."

"We still are. I will find a way for us to be together."

"Find a way to kill a zhombie?"

Fleming laughed bitterly. "I wouldn't have put it exactly like that." He kissed me, ever so softly, on the lips.

"You're my one and only, Fleming," I said, "I love you."

"And you are mine." He smiled. "Are you ready to go out so I can say goodbye to the others?"

"No."

"Silly." He took my hand for the last time and led me to the living room.

"There you are!" Barbara said. "We looked around and y'all were gone." She noticed the sadness on my face. "What's wrong?"

"Fleming has to go now."

"Oh no!"

"Fleming!"

"We thought you could stay!"

Everyone crowded around, speaking at once. Everyone but Cynthia and I. We held hands and watched.

"I've already told Lisa to get in a punch for me when you put Sharon away," Fleming said, "Cynthia, how about a hug? Would you mind?" She ran to him and threw her arms around his neck.

"Thank you," she whispered.

"You're welcome, honey." Fleming took a good look at her, memorizing her and turned to me. If zhombies had a heart, mine was definitely breaking. "Goodbye for now, my sweetheart," Fleming said sadly.

I grabbed him in a desperate hug. "If you don't come back for me, I'll kill you!"

Fleming chuckled. "That won't do us any good. We need to find a way to kill you, my darling."

I had to laugh.

"That's better," he said, "Remember I can come to you if you're in danger."

"The shared destiny thing?" I asked.

Fleming nodded.

"See you soon?"

"See you soon," came the answer and he was gone.

* * *

I must have looked as devastated as I felt because Barbara put her arms around me. "I need a break," I mumbled into her hair.

"What kind of break?"

"I dunno." I thought. I could call my caretaker and go have a long soak in my greenhouse tub...*No*. Too many memories. "Does anybody know what month this is?"

206

"It's January," Natalie answered.

Almost a year since my trip to see Sharon on the Old Coast Road. It seemed like centuries. Almost a year...I wonder? I looked out the window. The sun was up. When did that happen? "Can we go look for whales?"

"Whales?" Louise asked blankly.

"Uh-huh," Cynthia nodded. "The whales should be running."

"Where would you like to go to look for whales?" Barbara asked.

"Does this involve renting a boat?" Ric demanded.

"No," I sighed. "There's a turnout I know just north of here. There's a natural canyon under the water and the whales come in close to the cliff. Can we go there?"

Everyone looked at Ric.

"Yes, we can go since it doesn't involve renting a boat."

"What about protecting ourselves?" Rachel asked somewhat timidly.

I clenched my teeth. "Sharon is a pig fit for nothing but barbecuing and I'm the one to light the fire."

Barbara patted me on the back and smiled at Rachel. "I think she means she'll take her chances."

Ric tossed his keys in the air and caught them. "Shall we?"

We piled into Ric's SUV and drove north on Highway One. It was early, probably only around seven. The day was crystal clear and full of promise. The storm must have passed us by. There was no wind and the ocean was calm. Good day for whale watching. The sky was impossibly blue and the ocean even bluer. Iceplant was blooming and the hillsides were coated with yellow and neon pink. Hawks soared above us, calling to their breakfast. It was an incredible Big Sur day.

It didn't take long to reach my favorite turnout. Most people went right by it because it was tucked in a curve. It was only big enough to hold a couple of cars and Ric parked his monster so no one else could come in and disturb us. That thing was good for something after all. We perched on boulders and the guardrail with the winter sun on our backs. Cynthia swore she had seen a spout on the way up so we all had high hopes. We sat in silence and drank up the beauty.

"There's one!" yelled Ric.

"Where?" we shouted and jumped to our feet. Oh, sure enough! There went another spout and then another. Still a little far out, we couldn't see much but spouts. There's something so exciting about sighting whales.

"Come closer, come closer," Cynthia crooned.

"Swimming skyscrapers," Ric said.

I laughed. "Pretty close to it."

"I've never seen a whale," Louise said.

"Neither have I," said Rachel.

"Nor I," Barbara put in.

"How about you, Anna? Have you ever seen a whale?" I asked.

She shook her head solemnly. "No."

"Well, you're fixin' to!" I cried and pointed, "Look!"

Two California Grey whales cavorted in slow motion directly below us. They rolled, chased each other and slapped the water with their flukes. We could hear the magnificent *whoosh* of their breath as they spouted. I couldn't help myself, I jumped up and down and cheered. When I was human, tears used to run down my face, uncontrollable, whenever I saw the whales play.

And, as they had done for me on that day almost a year ago, the whales shouldered my pain. They helped me carry the burden somehow. "Thank you," I whispered.

I have no idea how long the whales stayed with us. The sun was higher in the sky when we turned to go. The whales had meandered off into open sea. We sat and talked in snatches about nothing at all and scanned for more whales. At long last, I stirred and said, "I'm ready now."

Each and every one of us knew what this meant.

It was time to take on Sharon.

We walked to the truck. Ric stopped as he was opening the driver's door and looked at us, gathered around. "To the cabin?"

Gazes met and locked with one intent.

"To the cabin," Anna said.

It was quiet in Ric's SUV during the drive south. Traffic had picked up and Ric had his hands full. The rest of us were in another world. I, for one, was having a talk with my other selves, making sure they were still with me.

We turned off Highway One and drove slowly toward the office and our cabin behind. A woman came out and flagged us down. Ric stopped and opened the driver's window.

"I'm going to have to ask you to leave. Our other guests complained about strange lights and noises coming from your cabin all night."

"We're too weird for Big Sur?" Ric asked incredulously.

"What?" the manager asked flatly, not amused.

"Nothing. We'll get out right away."

"I'd appreciate it if you'd drop the key off on your way out. That way, I know you're gone." She turned on her heel and marched back to the office.

"Trusting little soul," observed Barbara.

"Well," Rachel sighed, "Let's go clear out."

Truck loaded, bill paid and key returned, we sat at Highway One. Ric turned around in his seat. "Where to, ladies?"

Silence. The truck idled.

"I wonder if Sharon's home?" I asked.

"Oh, ho, ho," Barbara chuckled wickedly.

"Ooo," Natalie crooned.

"You are such a bad girl!" laughed Ric.

"Oh, *yes*," Louise exulted. "I do like the way you think!"

"Cynthia? Anna?" I asked, "Y'all are the only ones we haven't heard from."

"Let's go," Cynthia said.

Anna nodded. "Yep."

"Turn left, Ric," I directed. We pulled onto Highway One.

"Next stop, Pico Blanco."

Chapter Thirty

All was serene when we parked in front of Sharon's cabin. The water wheel *shushed*, light trickled through the redwoods and a Stellar's Jay called from a Pittosporum by the river. He flew across in front of us in a brilliant streak of blue and landed high in a redwood, chattering and alerting the forest to our arrival. It appeared no one was home. The green SUV was parked beside the cabin but the cabin was closed and shuttered. No smoke rose from the chimney.

"Nice place," Ric said admiringly.

"Too good for her," I said bitterly.

"We get rid of Sharon, we could probably buy this place on the courthouse steps," Ric remarked, opening his door.

"You mean buy it at auction?" I stuck a toe down, trying to find the ground.

"Just jump, Lisa, for crying out loud," Ric snapped, "It's not like you'll break."

"Oh yeah," I said sheepishly, hopping to the ground, "I keep forgetting."

"Immortal is as immortal does," Barbara said.

"What's that supposed to mean?" I started poking around the yard, snooping.

"I don't know," Barbara shrugged, "I just liked the way it sounded."

"Southerners!" I scoffed. "Ric, could we really buy this place at auction?"

"There's always the possibility." He tried to peek in a window. Curtains are drawn. I'd say our hostess isn't at home."

"I like it here," announced Anna, "It has horse corrals."

"What?" Cynthia and I cried together, "Where?"

"Over here." Anna led us to a nook in the redwoods on the east side of the cabin. There was a beautiful little meadow, small barn and a shed. It was obvious Sharon hadn't used it, the fences were a little tumbledown but with a relatively small amount of work, it could be a nice setup. Best of all, it was big enough for three horses. Well, two horses and a pony. I put my arm around Anna and she leaned into me. "We'll get him, Anna," I said, "We'll get Billy for you."

She sighed and looked at me with those incredible green eyes. "I know." She grinned. "I can't wait to see him again."

"Yeah, I can't wait to see Rosie and Traveler again."

"You have Rosie and Traveler?" asked Cynthia.

"Uh-huh," I nodded.

"For some reason, I thought they'd be dead."

I put my other arm around Cynthia. "They're very much alive, healthy and happy." I steered us back to the cabin. The others were poking around aimlessly. Ric straightened from trying to see in another window.

"What do we do, girls?" he asked.

I walked to the clearing where Sharon and I had sat before. "We form the *Circle*."

"With the intent of…?" asked Natalie.

"With the intent of introducing Sharon to her doom," I said darkly.

Ric laughed. "Look who's the drama queen now!" He grabbed Natalie's hand and pulled her to the clearing. "Come on, Nats."

"Don't call me Nats," she said automatically. She reached for Rachel. "Let's go, girl. Seriously, though, what is our intent?"

We call Sharon here and send her someplace, just like we did SoulJumper," I said impatiently.

Barbara took my hand and squeezed. "Calm down. Natalie's right. Send her where?"

"I think she should have to look at her ugly self all the time," Anna said.

"A mirror world?" Ric mused.

"So far, so good," I said, "Two dimensional, just like her." I thought for a second. "With no beauty parlors!"

Barbara chuckled. "Glad to see your sense of humor is returning."

"I'm serious!" I protested, only half joking. "Let her be un-permed and un-dyed for eternity!"

"We might be on to something with this mirror world," Rachel said. "When I was a little girl, I heard about this spell you could use for people who were doing bad things to you. Take a picture of them, put it face down on the mirror and seal it with black tape, so no light can get in. Then you bury it. Supposedly all the person's wickedness was mirrored back at them afterwards."

"Oh, I see where you're going with this," Ric said.

"What if we created something like that for her?"

"But Rachel, what's to keep her there?" Louise asked.

"If everything she does is mirrored back at her, it might work."

"Put her between two mirrors," Anna said.

"Then she'd be caught with everything bouncing back and forth into infinity!" Ric crowed.

"Seal it with…?" I asked.

"Darkness," Anna said distinctly.

"Darkness it is." I smiled at her. She definitely had gumption.

"All right, we've got a mirror world – flat?" Ric looked at me. I nodded. "Okay, flat. Two mirrors, facing each other, sealed with darkness. Anything else?"

"No access to anything," Cynthia said, "No outside input, no energy."

"Stuck with herself," said Louise grimly.

"Is that it?" Ric looked around the *Circle*. "Nothing to add? Anyone?" No answer. "Grab hold, then."

We didn't clasp in one by one this time and we didn't each state our intent. We visualized our intent in its entirety.

When we clasped in, I saw endless *Maternal Circles of Power* with endless arrays of 'us' in them. All clasping at once. Alternate realities. In every direction; past, present and future. In each one, variations of ourselves doing exactly the same thing.

So *that* was her ace in the hole.

I think it blew up in her face.

Universal synchronicity.

In every reality Sharon had infiltrated and created zhombies of us, no matter how divergent, different versions of us clasped into the *Maternal Circle*. I saw hands, all at exactly the same instant, close around each other with a sound like a celestial bell. In each world, endless versions of ourselves envisioned exactly the same thing.

A mirror world for Sharon, made of two mirrors facing each other, sealed with darkness nothing could penetrate.

In every reality, Sharon appeared at the center of the *Circle*. Stripped of any humanity, she resembled a huge worm with a bulbous head. Her pink flesh mottled purple with anger, she bobbed her head at us and hissed. Tiny arms flailed uselessly. She darted at us on short, misshapen legs, snarling and snapping.

The real Sharon, at last.

In hundreds of worlds, our very souls pushed her up and up. The power she had stolen for so long carried her to her prison, wailing like a banshee. Who knew what she originally was, if she ever had been human. All those realities, all those minds, all those *Maternal Circles of Power* with one single intent.

I heard one last bloodcurdling scream. "This one's for you, Fleming," I thought as Sharon's mirror world sealed with a reverberating boom. I hoped it echoed forever in there.

The alternate realities stayed until, with one motion, hundreds of hands unclasped at exactly the same moment. I sent a mental *thank you* to them.

We stood under the Redwood trees, listening to the Little Sur River chuckle and the water wheel go *shushshushshush* and knew we were finally free.

Could you believe that?" Natalie asked breathlessly.

"You saw it, too?" I cried.

"I think we all did," said Ric.

"How many realities do you think...?" Rachel ran out of steam.

"Lots," said Anna.

"How dare she?" Barbara huffed.

"That was definitely what she thought she had over us," Louise said.

"Can you believe we all had the same idea at once?" I asked.

"Now that is what's remarkable," Ric said, "I honestly don't know if we could have taken her out alone."

"All those realities rebelled at once," Cynthia said, awed. "I can't get over it!"

"I'll tell you what I can't get over," I said. My dear family stopped talking and looked expectantly at me.

"*We're free!*"

* * *

We had ourselves a little celebration, there at Sharon's house, dancing and cavorting. That escalated into hopping in the river in the deep pool above the water wheel and splashing each other giddily. We bathed ourselves clean of sexual slavery in the sparkling Little Sur River with the redwoods whispering a benediction. We laid in patches of intensely green shamrocks with the sun filtering down to dry us off. Calming down at last, we talked lazily about pretty much everything. We went over and over the experience of seeing our alternate realities, still amazed at the synchronicity.

We talked about the future and what we wanted to do with it. For now, we would all live at Ric's in Big Sur. I volunteered to sell my farm so we could buy Sharon's place if there was a possibility. Anna chattered about seeing Billy.

At length, we wound down and lay with the shamrocks around our ears, silent. It was starting to look like late afternoon from the shadows when Natalie stirred and suggested we leave. "Let's just go to your house, Ric. Who cares if there's plywood nailed over the windows? We can walk outside if we want to see the view."

"I agree," said Barbara, "I'm sick of being a vagabond."

Before we loaded up in Ric's truck, I stopped to say a final goodbye to the place on Pico Blanco. Ric hesitated beside me, understanding. "Don't worry," he said, "We have to buy it now."

"Why is that?"

"It's the site of our emancipation!" he shouted gleefully.

"Nut," I said affectionately. "Get in the truck. The sooner we get to your house, the sooner we can find out if she owned it."

"Right-o." Ric hopped in the driver's seat. "All abo-oard!"

We drove out of the shadows under the redwoods into brilliant sunlight in our faces. The sun was setting over the Pacific.

"Look!" Cynthia cried, pointing.

A whale spouted, then more and more. We counted eight spouts that beautiful evening. One for each of us.

The whales welcomed us home.

* * *

Ric's house wasn't too bad. Big sheets of plywood were nailed over the windows and the holes in the roof. A cleaning crew had gotten up the mess inside. There was still drywall missing in spots but it was do-able. The first thing I did was check to see if I could build us a fire. Everything looked intact, so I built us a ripsnorter. We gathered in front of it.

Ric made coffee and munchies and we had a food celebration. He was right, sharing food did create closeness. We still had that, even if we couldn't taste it. We sat around the fire that entire night, reliving the moment when we saw the alternate realities. From time to time we wandered outside and looked at the stars.

When the sun rose, we were gathered on the cliff above the ocean, watching the first day of our freedom dawn.

Epilogue

We got Ric's house fixed up quickly and lived there together. It turned out Sharon had rented her place, so Ric had his agent contact the owner. She was happy to sell at the price Ric offered and within six months, we lived at the cabin on Pico Blanc as well.

When Ric got a chance to go back to St. Simon's Island to check on his house, he discovered it had burned the night we ran into SoulJumper there. After a family conference, we decided to rebuild and our new house will soon be finished. Then we'll be bi-coastal zhombies.

Cynthia and Louise are inseparable. That relationship bloomed. Lonely as we all are, we're happy for those two.

I never sold my farm. Ric said he had plenty without us doing that and we brought Billy there for Anna. Seasoned as were now, it was a simple procedure. They had quite the reunion and he was happy living with Rosie and Traveler. As soon as we got the place on Pico Blanco, I leased out my farm and we brought the horses to Big Sur. I just couldn't bear to go back to Carmel Valley.

I haven't heard anything from Fleming since he helped us reunite ourselves. I never go through a single day without thinking of him and missing him.

And hoping that somehow, someday, he'll find a way to kill a zhombie.

THE END